"I want to make love to you."

He was just barely tasting her lips, inhaling the fragrance of her hair and skin. "You're in a tough spot, Miss Hamilton."

"And you're no gentleman." Georgina said raggedly.

"I thought I was being rather gallant." Quinn was exploring her mouth deeply, forcing her to meet his passion with her own. His desire to possess her was sweeping him on.

"Quinn!" She dragged her mouth away. She looked startlingly beautiful and utterly desirable. "If you think I'm a pushover, you've got another think coming."

He, too, looked different, the bold striking face carved into severity. "Are you *afraid* to tangle with me?"

"You know I am." She didn't say it nervously, or provocatively, but with a grave sincerity, and he answered with a mocking bow.

A Place Called Rambulara

Margaret Way

Harlequin Books

TORONTO • NEW YORK • LONDON
AMSTERDAM • PARIS • SYDNEY • HAMBURG
STOCKHOLM • ATHENS • TOKYO • MILAN

Original hardcover edition published in 1984
by Mills & Boon Limited

ISBN 0-373-02658-7

Harlequin Romance first edition November 1984

CHAPTER ONE

THERE were several letters waiting for Georgina when she arrived home. She sorted through them quickly, dismissed the bills promptly and carried the only one of interest into the living room. It was from Richard. His writing wasn't much of an improvement on his merry five-year-old's, all big loops and funny squiggles.

'Georgie darling,' the letter began, and Georgina found herself snorting derisively. Whenever Richard addressed her as 'Georgie darling' she could be sure he was about to land her with a problem, but her love for him couldn't allow that to deter her. She resisted the notion to pour herself a stiff drink and sank down into an armchair, reading on compulsively.

Revelation followed revelation. Jilly's strange moods, bouts of jealousy and hysteria, how she had become untidy and was losing her figure, the way she shouted at the children and criticised him constantly, her crazy sense of persecution, his perfectly understandable dismay and bewilderment. Georgina could see it all clearly; Jilly the hapless neurotic, Richard the innocent husband. There was so much of it, Georgina wanted to curse aloud. She loved her brother, *loved* him, but unlike Jilly at the beginning she was never blind to his faults. Worries about Richard and Jilly were ever present in her mind. But still, to read that Jilly had run off and left him was extraordinarily shocking. Jilly was so much stronger than Richard, a wonderfully dedicated little wife and mother. Or so Georgina had thought.

She re-read the letter with grieved astonishment. Such was her concentration, she bit deeply on her beautifully moulded bottom lip. It was all as she feared. Jilly had not only left her husband, but more awfully, her two

babies. Though they wouldn't be babies really. Tim
would be nearly four, adorable little Timmy with his
red-brown hair and glowing eyes, and Missy—Melissa,
a radiant two and a bit. She moaned with frustration at
not being able to rush and comfort them. At least one
could understand Jilly's desire to give Richard a good
fright, but running off and leaving those two!

Georgina had a vivid mental picture of two tear-
stained little faces surrounded by bright curls. The
whole thing was crazy. Jilly couldn't live without
Richard, much less her little ones. She had the most
generous, loving, trampled-on heart in the world. Her
fate had been sealed at the tender age of eighteen when
she had looked into Richard's blazing, daring, bold
topaz eyes.

'What have you *done* to her?' Georgina suddenly
cried aloud. She was extremely fond of her sister-in-law
and invariably on Jilly's side, as any fair-minded person
would have to be. Richard in many ways was a very
fetching creature, but not even his sister could call him
a stalwart type. All life was a game. He had made that
perfectly clear from the cradle.

Georgina folded the letter not once but several times.
Sexual attraction was a very dangerous thing. Here
were two young people, married at eighteen (despite her
cautionary comments) on the sole grounds that they
greatly fancied each other, and now a few short years
later Jilly had up and left without apology. She must
have been tried beyond her limits, that was it. If she had
left Richard and the children, it was because he had
somehow succeeded in turning her whole world upside
down. Jilly had been mad about Richard right up until
a month ago when Georgina had received her last letter.
Richard had lost interest in growing the avocados that
were going to make him a fortune, turned his back on
the lush coastal strip and dragged his family Outback—
the real Australia, he had told his sister as she was
trying to dry her eyes. She had loved being an aunt,
loved having Jilly for a friend, but Richard had moved

them to some godforsaken station in the Outback. A place called Rambulara, one of those curiously awesome pastoral holdings where single families sat on a million acres.

Georgina jumped up in a fury, thinking she would have that drink. What this last letter amounted to was a mystery. Both Richard and Jilly had written often of their new home. Possibly in excessively glowing terms ... the savage splendour, the way the sun moved across the blood-red desert pyramids, the fascination of the blue mirage, the immensity of the ancient land, a whirlwind trip they had made into the Dead Heart. It couldn't possibly be as exotic as all that, Georgina thought after several sips of her drink. Not with drought ever-present. Sometimes, Jilly had written, the sky was filled with green clouds, millions of little budgies in an ecstasy of flight.

It was so hot Georgina opened the top button of her silk shirt. Ever the journalist, she thought briefly of a series of articles about the Dead Heart. In little over a month's time, the Prince and Princess of Wales were making an historic visit to Alice Springs. The heir to a thousand years of British history perhaps to climb the six-hundred-million-years-old Ayers Rock? Georgina had always had a soft spot for Prince Charles, even now when he was happily married to a positively super girl. It should be a brilliant time. Probably the whole Centre would go wild, and why not? The British Royal Family were living proof that the people cherished the kind of rulers who lived and breathed dedication to their high office. And how unexpected that little English Jilly should run off at such a time. She, who loved the Royal Family like her own. It didn't make sense.

Georgina went back to Richard's letter. 'I know I've always been able to count on you, Georgie, one hundred per cent.'

Wasn't that the truth! How like Rick to readily suppose she could just drop her job and hare out to him ... 'I told the boss I had a sister who could help me

out'. . . . Georgina suddenly turned and crunched the
letter up. No matter the helpless rage in her, she and her
brother were inextricably linked, a tightly knit little
family of two since their parents had been tragically
killed when they were both still at high school.
Georgina still couldn't allow her mind to dwell on that
painful period. Her grief had been so terrible she had
had to shut it off to survive, not only for herself, but for
her young brother. The young Richard would never
have withstood the shock without her. She had heard
him, so often, tell people that when describing their
early years. Richard was still powerfully attached to
her, as she was to him. Very occasionally, as now,
Georgina found it a terrible burden. She would have to
go, if only for a few weeks. Richard and Jilly simply *had*
to patch things up. Keeping their marriage, their family
together was all-important. Obviously Jilly was suffering
some mental stress. Perhaps out there at that
godforsaken place she was too shut off from the kind of
life she was used to. And yet Georgina had her fears
that it was something that Richard had done.

She picked up a photograph from a side table and
stared down at it for a long time. Rick's familiar eyes,
topaz like her own, smiled back at her. They both had
those eyes, their mother's eyes; long, almond-shaped,
that strange, burnished colour. Their noses were the
same, the high cheekbones, the same wide, curvy
mouths. Georgina had spent a lot of time assuring
people they weren't twins. Both of them were tall, long-
limbed and graceful and both of them had a shock of
tawny hair. At least she wore hers long and beautifully
shaped. Richard often tended to look like a wild-eyed
saint, his sights always far afield, while she had always
to worry about the everyday things that kept them alive
and together. Jilly was beside him, so touchingly young
and pretty. A plump baby, Timmy, was saddled on her
slim hip. Too young to be parents, Georgina had
always thought—more a lack of maturity than actual
years. The answer now seemed clear. They had

compounded too much into too short a time. It was a big thing working out relationships, and Jilly's strength would be depleted with two children under five.

Georgina held the photograph at arm's length as tears rushed into her eyes. There was no question that she was on Jilly's side, and she realised her sister-in-law had no one in the whole country to turn to. Jilly, too, was almost an orphan, for she had lost her own mother when she was almost eight and when her father remarried a few years later her stepmother had been discomfited by a ready-made child. Family strains, in fact, had set Jilly on her travels and in that crucial period of her life she had met and swiftly married the Richard she had instantly adored ... 'Why, Georgie, he's as bright and beautiful as an archangel!' He was handsome all right, Georgina thought grimly; would that he were more striving and stolid. Perhaps a little of it was her fault. She had taken too much of the load, attempting to alleviate her young brother's loss when she should have let him try. Richard had become used to intense self-sacrifice from his women, but at least one had jacked up.

CHAPTER TWO

JILLY *had* run away. To her.

When Georgina opened her front door the next morning, she got the shock of her life. She couldn't even speak first.

'Oh, Georgie!' As she spoke Jilly hurled herself at her sister-in-law, her deep blue-violet eyes swimming with tears.

'It's *you*, Jilly,' Georgina said flatly, clutching at the girl. What had happened to Jilly? Where had her fair prettiness vanished to? What had happened to that glorious English skin, the petite figure? 'My *dear*!' she sighed in an agonised exclamation.

'I had to come to you, Georgie. I've no one else.'

'Of course, of course. Come in, Jilly. Come in and sit down.' Georgina had both arms fully occupied, so she actually kicked the door shut. 'Have you eaten? Have you had breakfast?' She tried to look into Jilly's face, but it was all but obscured by a long, lank tangle of honey-coloured hair.

'I've left Rick,' Jilly gasped.

'I'm terribly sorry, dear—I know.' Georgina was only a year older than her brother and sister-in-law, yet she invariably spoke to them both like a doting maiden aunt. She imagined it was because both of them made her feel very old and wise. 'Here, I'm going to make us a cup of tea,' she said comfortingly. 'No, don't sit alone in an empty room,' she supported the sagging Jilly, 'come into the kitchen.'

'Oh, Georgie!' her sister-in-law wailed again. 'What a lovely person you are! To think you could have such a frightful brother!'

'Don't worry, dear, I won't let him break your heart.' Georgina pressed her sister-in-law down into a chair.

10

'He's written to me, of course.'

'I'll bet he has!' Jilly aroused herself briefly. 'He's always leaned on you, hasn't he? Ever since you lost your parents.'

'I think that had a lot to do with the way Rick is,' said Georgina in a gentle voice. 'It's impossible not to be affected.'

'Oh, yes, yes,' Jilly reached out and caught Georgina's hand, 'I know that, Georgie, but it made *you* strong.'

'Ah, but we women have to be strong, don't we?' Georgina made a wry little face. 'It's the male who's fussed over from the cradle.'

'Tell me about it,' Jilly said bleakly, picturing her stepbrother. 'Whatever Richard is,' she said rigidly, obviously struggling with tears, 'I've always felt he loved me.'

'He *does* love you.' Georgina leaned heavily against the table.

'No.' Jilly bowed her head and broke down.

It was terribly distressing, and Georgina quietly took a seat beside her, constantly patting Jilly's head. At one point she thought Jilly was going to make herself ill, but gradually she calmed.

'Sorry about that,' she hiccuped.

'I expect it helps to cry it out.'

'You've always been immensely comforting,' Jilly trembled. 'Remember how it was you who had to care for me when Timmy was arriving? Rick was in a typical state of shock.'

'Like so many first-time fathers,' Georgina tried to smile. 'What has he done to you? Tell me.'

'I should have realised I'd never be enough for him,' Jilly sighed.

'Jilly!' Whatever Georgina had been wondering, it wasn't this.

'She's only amusing herself,' Jilly observed, trying to sound cynical, but sounding devastated instead. 'But my poor silly husband thinks that she's in love with him. In love with *Rick*, when it's her own brother-in-law she's after!'

Georgina's exhaled breath whistled through her teeth. 'I think you'd better start at the beginning,' she said. 'Meanwhile I'll make the breakfast.'

And so it all came out.

'I can't believe this!' Georgina exclaimed repeatedly, and shook her head. Richard, for all his handsomeness, was the victim of a terribly unconscious allure. He was no womaniser, his sister was sure of that. Why, for a long time he had used to cringe if a girl so much as looked at him too hard or too long. Richard's idea of a wonderful time had always been the all-male activities, football, cricket, riding the waves or his wonderful, wretched bike.

'I don't seem to remember your mentioning this woman,' she told Jilly, and moved the salt and pepper shakers nearer her hand.

'Maybe I wanted to pretend she wasn't really there,' Jilly mumbled. 'Does she just want my Rick because he's beautiful?'

'I think I'll have to get out there to answer that. But surely if she wants her own brother-in-law and your employer it makes everything so much more dangerous?'

'I don't know what she's up to,' Jilly said, and dried her eyes. 'Maybe she's trying to make Quinn jealous.'

'Why?'

'Of course you don't know Quinn,' said Jilly. 'He's terribly, terribly important and self-contained. He could have any woman he wanted any old time, but I don't think he finds us terribly important.'

'Really?' Georgina sniffed her hostility, but Jilly only said calmly:

'It's a man's world out there. I'll bet you've never met anyone like Quinn Shieffield in your life. In some ways they live like Royalty, in palaces with enough land for a small country and everyone looking up to them and admiring them. And they're so rich! Everyone in the Outback knows the Shieffields. They're famous.'

'They must be charming,' Georgina said drily.

Jilly actually smiled, and a little colour came to her pale cheeks. 'Well, we both know how beautiful Rick is, but he's not a patch on the Boss. Quinn is a *man*, an empire-builder. They still exist. Beside Quinn, Rick is a mischievous, ineffectual boy—especially now when he's allowing Lucinda to make such a fool of him.'

Georgina shook her tawny head, in the bright light of morning a genuine, if not a classic beauty. Hers was a modern face, full of spirit and character, the rarity of her tawny colouring lending her an extraordinary vividness.

'Sure you're not a little in love with this Quinn Shieffield yourself?' she queried.

'Goodness me, *no!*' Jilly blinked. 'I'm a married woman, though I can't be sure for how long and even if I wasn't, I'd never qualify for that honour. I tell you, you've no idea how these Shieffields live. Quinn would only marry someone from his own world.'

'Jolly good!' Georgina enthused mockingly. 'How come this paragon isn't married yet?'

'He might if he'd take some time off from the station, but it's so huge.'

'And I gather this Lucinda is working at drawing his eye?'

'She was engaged to him once,' Jilly explained.

'Good grief!'

Jilly sighed deeply and within herself. 'Not long after it was broken off she and Quinn's younger brother, David, ran off and got married. It must have been blighted from the start. I've heard they were desperately unhappy, and of course David Shieffield was killed in some crazy stunt flying his plane as low as possible over the property. Some people say he meant to die.' Jilly's blue eyes were grave and remote.

'And how long ago was this?' asked Georgina.

'Three years.' Jilly's small hands shook. 'For

someone who devours her own brother-in-law with her eyes Lucinda is playing a peculiar game.'

'Maybe she's a nymphomaniac?' Georgina's clear, vibrant voice took on a sharp note.

'I don't know what she is,' Jilly mourned, her small face puckering with distress. 'She treats me with contempt, yet she comes round after my husband.'

'Ever thought of throwing her out?'

'She's a *Shieffield!*' Jilly gasped, as though that counted for everything.

'And does that give her the right to break up your marriage—if indeed that's what she's trying to do?'

'Who knows what's on her mind?' Jilly cried, and looked at her sister-in-law beseechingly. 'Besides, Rick is tired of me. I could never understand why he married me in the first place. I'm so ordinary!'

Georgina squeezed her arm. 'You must know you have such a lot going for you. You're everything Rick needs, even if he's falling down on the job.'

'I'm fat!' Jilly wailed, starting to cry again. 'I used to be so trim, too.'

'There, there, a few pounds. . . .'

'A stone and a bit.' Jilly allowed her sister-in-law to continue rubbing her back. 'I never thought I'd succumb to food, but I have. I get so strung-up, I just have to eat.'

'Don't sound so guilty, dear. Lots of people do. I feel it's a small thing for you to get your figure back, but first you have to sort yourself out. Are you sure Rick is having an affair with this Shieffield woman?'

'I think so.'

'You mean you didn't ask straight out?'

'I couldn't bring myself to,' Jilly confessed.

'Good grief, Jilly!' Georgina heaved herself to her feet. 'You mean you've got yourself in this state and you don't really *know?*'

'Yes, I'm sure.' Jilly amended abruptly. 'You only have to see Rick look at her.'

'And what does he look like?'

'Miserable. And excited.'

'And what does *she* look like?' asked Georgina.

'Like a rotten snake with a rabbit.'

'Heavens!' Georgina knew a moment of pure horror. She supposed Rick might be easily hypnotised at that.

'She thinks she's so beautiful, yet there's something sly about her. All sorts of odd emotions flow about when she's there. She's supposed to be a lady, with her rich family and her lovely clothes, but I think she's sort of . . . wild. You should see her ride! You'd think she'd set her mind to fly!'

'Doesn't she have a home of her own, then?' Georgina asked.

'Oh yes, but she's virtually abandoned it for Rambulara. I think she's been after it all her life. And Quinn. But somehow Quinn got away.'

'And what does this shrieking creature of passion look like?' Georgina asked.

'Fabulous,' Jilly said unhappily, and closed her eyes. 'Her hair and eyes are jet black and she has this very white skin. It's a sinister kind of beauty, not bright and shining like you. Your mouth always looks as if it's going to smile, but Lucinda's is always thin, with a kind of delicate sneer. Missy shrinks away from her and Tim doesn't know why, but he's filled with hostility and aggression. I guess both children sense that she's making their mother very unhappy.'

'But after all, dear,' Georgina turned around, 'you should have had this out and cleared the air. Rick never once mentioned her in his letter.'

'He wouldn't, the cowardly monster!'

Georgina settled herself down in her chair again. 'Maybe he's a bit of a coward, but I can't see him as a heartless monster. He does love you, Jilly. He said having you in his life was like always having the sun on his face. You're very important to him. He adores the children. Given his rather restless temperament, he's doing his best to make a good father. Then suddenly this *femme fatale* comes along. It sounds to me as if she set out to attract his attention.'

'She did.' Jilly's blue eyes flashed like sapphires.

'But you know for certain she's not serious?'

'Oh, no. It's Quinn she wants.' Jilly drank deeply on her third cup of tea. 'But Quinn refused her, even if he sometimes remembers.'

'Do you think he could marry her?' Georgina asked.

'One of the men told Rick he wouldn't think of it. A man can't marry his brother's widow. But there's something between them, some kind of thrill in the air that's almost palpable. Both of them are so . . . powerful. That's why I was so astonished when she started to speak to Rick. I mean, Rick may be dazzling in his own way, but he's a young, married employee. She can't bring herself to speak to Mick Donovan, and he's the overseer.'

'I think Rick is a fool,' Georgina said suddenly. 'We'll have to go out there just as soon as we can.'

'Not me, Georgie,' Jilly shuddered. 'I've had as much as I can take. It's breaking my heart to leave the children, but Rick loves them and I guess he'll be too busy looking after them to think about Lucinda.'

'But Jilly, you know perfectly well you can't leave them. Rick has his work to do.'

'Can't *you* go out?' Jilly begged her. 'You're such a vivid, positive person, you'll see it all the way it is. You'll be able to speak to Rick, reason with him. The children will dance with happiness to have you.' Jilly's small pale face wore an expression of acute suffering. 'I can't take any more, Georgie, I *can't*!'

'All right, dear.' Georgina recognised that this was indeed true. 'You're obviously in a very depressed state, and you have reason to be. I feel a holiday will transform you. *I* can turn Rick around. You do want him turned around, don't you?'

'Who else have I got?' Jilly asked bleakly. 'Losing your man undermines all your self-esteem.'

'You haven't lost him, Jilly, that's ridiculous. Rick never once mentioned any thought of a separation.'

'Of course not. He needs me for the children, while he concentrates his attention on that scheming woman. I'm just the housekeeper now, someone to take care of him and them. I'm not a person with needs of my own. No one has to take care of *me*.'

'*You* have to take care of you,' Georgina said firmly.

Jilly looked down at herself ruefully. 'Say it—I've let myself go. It's really sad, isn't it, an unhappy woman's dependency on food?'

Georgina smiled. 'I can't think of many who don't dearly love food. Pretty well all of us have to accept that we can't eat as we like. It's a little harder again when one has a small frame.'

'You have such a beautiful figure, Georgie,' Jilly pointed out.

'I'm a bit of a health nut. I get a lot of exercise and try to eat the right things. Perhaps part of the problem, Jilly, is getting back into shape after Melissa.'

'I suppose so. It wasn't as easy as after Tim.'

'I think a holiday and some new clothes would give you a huge lift,' said Georgina. 'Believe me when I say this unhappy period will pass away. I know Rick, Jilly. If he really loved this woman he would have told me. Maybe he's suffering from some stupid infatuation, but it will grind inexorably to a halt. As it's so important to you, I'll get out there. But I don't know for how long. I've got plenty of leave, of course, but it's not always convenient to fit it in.'

'Oh, try, Georgie! If you can't help me, I just might have to fling myself under a bus!' wailed Jilly.

'Don't do that, dear,' Georgina kissed her sister-in-law's cheek gently, 'it would be too messy. No, the thing to do is get back to your old self.'

Jilly touched her eyes and more tears started to fall. 'That will be difficult. I haven't got much money.'

'No, but I've got enough to lend you.' Georgina covered one small, work-roughened hand with her own. 'Don't worry about spending it either—I'll get it back from Rick. Now, let's plan this. You can stay here.

You'll have the house and the use of the car and you can take off to the beach any time you like. You always did love the surf.'

'Oh, Geórgie!' Jilly was overcome by such goodness.

'The thing is, I don't think I could manage any more than a month at the outside,' Georgina warned.

'I couldn't either,' Jilly confirmed. She raised her lovely, tragic eyes and mopped them with a Kleenex. They were her only asset undiminished by her trials. However unhappy a woman became, Georgina reflected deeply, she couldn't afford to stop working on her appearance. In the general way men didn't suffer the same physical ravages. It was wickedly unfair!

The offices for *Profile* magazine were in an incredibly seedy-looking building down a narrow lane. When the wind was blowing, floating little bits of grubby paper, Georgina used to put her handbag up to protect her face, but she had never allowed her daunting place of business to depress her. Not even on that first day when, fresh out of university with a major in journalism, she had applied anxiously for a lowly job. Years of working nights and weekends at waitressing or whatever odd job was offering had cured her of undue alarms and actually added to her powers of expression. Once she had tipped the entire contents of her drinks tray on a guest's head, slipping in her opinion of him at the same time. She had expected to be ushered to the door, but her employer, a restaurateur, had actually laughed. 'He deserved it, Georgie,' he had crowed. 'The whole thing was too delicious for words!' So many people had been kind to her when they came to realise she and Rick were on their own. Especially Max, her boss.

When Georgina walked into his office that morning, his face lit up. 'You're a wonderful girl, Georgie Hamilton. You know that?'

'You liked my little interview with Professor Bailey?'

'I've just finished it. It's great! I really mean that. You

have such a fresh, original approach. Who else but you could make that man warm and human?'

'But he is,' Georgina said quite seriously. 'I'm betting a big part of his rather grim image is shyness. Why, he told me the funniest things. I promised not to print them, of course.'

'This is terrific,' cried Max with complete confidence. 'I'll have you go along with Jeff so we'll get the photograph just right. With this kind of text we just might turn him into a sex symbol.'

'He should come up well,' Georgina noted. 'He's a fine-looking man and he looks completely different when he smiles.'

'Get him to smile, then,' Max urged her.

'That's what I want to talk to you about, Max,' she said, and looked at him pleadingly.

'Oh, my God, what? Not Rick again?' Max Duncan, a big burly man in his mid-forties, sat down heavily and thrust his glasses back on his nose.

'Are you psychic or something, Max?' Georgina asked.

'Sure I'm psychic, just like my old grannie, even if your face wasn't a dead give-away. How many years have you been working for me now, Georgie?'

She took a deep breath and answered, 'Four.'

'And how many times have you had to rescue your brother from some feckless escapade?'

'Oh, come on, Max,' she said a little wearily, 'there's no harm in Richard, you know that. He just took a little longer than most young men to mature.'

'You should never have allowed him to get married,' said Max, and stretched out in his chair.

'I couldn't stop him,' she pointed out.

'No—nice little thing, his wife, but just a couple of kids!'

Georgina bowed her tawny head in response. 'She's left him, Max.'

'By what means? I thought they were adventuring through the Interior?'

'They settled—I told you that.'

'Ah, yes. On a cattle station, wasn't it?'

'Yes, some place called Rambulara.'

'Sounds familiar,' Max frowned. 'Surely it's in that *Historic Homesteads of Australia*?'

'It could be,' Georgina shrugged. 'I'll look it up. The thing is, Jill is as down as possible without being ill, and she's come to me.'

'Why not?' Max laughed flatly. 'You're the mother figure in both those kids' lives, and God damn it, you're their age!'

'A year older.' Georgina gave it enough weight for a decade.

'So what does she want you to do, arrange a divorce?'

Georgina looked shocked. 'She loves him, Max! She adores the children.'

'And yet she succumbed to the urge to run away?' Max snorted.

'I know she acted in a state of shock. She thinks Rick is being unfaithful to her.'

'My God! Then again, why not? I don't remember seeing two better-looking youngsters than you two. Your sister-in-law must have realised she was going to have problems with Rick when she married him. He may not have your I.Q. or your character, but he sure is one good-looking guy. He could make a small fortune out of it, now that I think of it.'

'Rick's not like that, Max.' Georgina shook her head. 'He could never accept or cope with a sex-symbol tag. His good looks don't mean anything to him.'

'Maybe, but they're sure going to move the ladies. I thought that's why they went to live in the back of beyond?'

'No, Rick just felt like a change of scene. He's very restless.'

'So what is it you're asking of me?' Max asked. 'I'm not in the habit of granting favours.'

'What about some leave?' There was a breathless rush to Georgina's request.

'How long?' Max grunted.

'A month?'

'Nonsense!'

'All right, three weeks.'

'You're asking at the wrong time, Georgina,' Max said quite sharply. 'I intended sending you out to. . . .' He looked up at her with a searching frown. 'Where is this place, Rambulara?'

'Out west somewhere. Channel Country.'

'You mean a hop, step and a jump to the Alice?'

'I imagine so. It's a pretty big country.'

'You wouldn't know how big until you get out there, girlie,' Max assured her. 'The Outback is awesome. Do you mean to tell me you've never seen Ayers Rock or the Olgas?'

'Gosh, Max, you said it yourself. They're so far away. I've always meant to. . . .'

'Those *huge* stations!' Max interrupted her, obviously off on some train of thought.

'I believe Rambulara is round about a million acres,' Georgina said helpfully.

'Get the book for me, will you?' Max suddenly straightened up. 'If we haven't got it, run out and buy it. We just might be able to work out something. Kill two birds with the one stone. Something is jogging my memory about that place. Ram . . . bu . . . lara. . . .' He rolled it out on his tongue, then shut his eyes. 'I tell you, girl, the scenery alone is a lifetime experience. The red cliffs, the crystal clear waterholes, those fabulous desert gardens . . . those pioneering families still have a fascination for us folks. In a few weeks the Royals arrive. I was considering giving you a little reward. . . .'

'You mean I could go out?' Georgina struck her hands together.

'I said I was only considering. Marion is my senior feature writer.'

'Perhaps she'll need an assistant?'

'I'll think about it,' was all Max said. 'Just get me that book.'

Georgina had to walk two blocks to a bookstore to get it, and it wasn't cheap. 'Trying to impress someone, are you?' the salesgirl asked.

'Very much, actually. My boss.'

She was a little slower getting back to the office because the book was large and quite heavy.

'Oh, great,' said Max, putting a cup of coffee down on his desk. 'Would you like some?'

'Yes, please.' Georgina was a little tired and her face must have shown it.

'Debby can get it.' He went to the door and yelled. 'Now, show me this place.'

Georgina tore off the wrapping and opened the book at the index. 'Let's see ... Elizabeth Farm, Denbigh, Woolmers, Panshanger, Malahide ... ah, here it is: Rambulara, Queensland.' She turned carefully to the page.

'Blimey!' muttered Max. 'And Richard works there?'

'In a very lowly capacity, station hand.' Georgina began reading. 'To visit Rambulara is an unique experience . . .'

'*Shieffield*—of course!' Max put a finger down on the Shieffield family arms. 'Now I remember. One of the Shieffields married Lucinda Hallett—you know, *Hallett*. He was a one-time big grazier, now he's involved in everything—mining, real estate, even tropical fruits. We let them fall on the ground while they pay a fortune for them in places like Hong Kong. Anyway, it was never confirmed, but they say the Shieffield she married took a dive—literally. He crashed in his own plane.'

'Yes, I know.' Georgina was still reading.

'Here's your coffee, Georgina,' Debby, the young office assistant came through the door.

'Thanks, Deb. Could you put it down here?'

Debby glanced over Georgina's shoulder curiously. 'What are you looking at?'

'One of our very grand historic homesteads.'

'*Wow!*' Debby giggled. 'Are you going out there?'

'If Mr Duncan lets me go.'

'Lucky devil!' Debby's envious face was a study. 'You might catch yourself a rich grazier.'

'Yes, yes,' Max interrupted testily. 'Thank you, Debby.'

'They must have an extraordinary lifestyle,' said Georgina, studying the front view of the three-storey mansion. 'What do you suppose it would cost to build a house like this these days?'

'Millions—absolute millions,' said Max. 'Houses like this belong to another era. The Australian equivalent of the British castle. They were all built by British settlers who saw the chance to carve out empires in the new colonies. They had the capital, the education, the enormous resourcefulness and the vision. As you can see, the Hon George Arthur Shieffield established a great station that's still in his family's hands. Can you imagine what a challenge it must have been? A young man who was probably used to a brilliant society and pampered to boot, leaving it all behind and undertaking to impose his own kind of civilisation on the wilds?'

'Obviously he *did* it.' Georgina was studying further pictures of a grand staircase and a wonderful overhanging gallery adorned with arched columns. 'He must have been a gloriously strong and capable gentleman.'

Max turned his head to study her rapt profile. Was it her colouring that gave her that odd radiance, or was it her essential purity shining forth? An old-fashioned word, but Max thought it still applied. Georgina was a good girl, a complete person, unlike the charming, haphazard brother she so loved. What appeared to have happened was that their parents had been killed at the worst possible time for the boy. Georgina had done all and more than could possibly have been expected of her, but a woman couldn't completely take a man's place. The boy needed his father—a man's discipline, the male identification, the knowledge that someone was going to see him toe the line or else. Georgina had been unable to press her expectations of her brother as a parent would and he had refused point blank to undertake tertiary study when he left school. Georgina had been the anchor, he had been the restless drifter— not that there was anything seriously wrong with the boy. Circumstances, when one thought about it. The terrible tragedy of losing both parents. Yet Georgina had tried so hard for him.

'Well, I guess I can spare you for a month,' Max said at last. 'Anyway, there are a few things you can do out there. Interview Shieffield, for one. The modus operandi of a cattle baron. People like to sit back and read about people like that. Let's see what you can do with an article about the Outback and its people. How they're standing up to the drought. I said Marion will cover the Royals on their visit, but I thought you might be good telling us how the people of the Centre are looking forward to this historic visit. You're as good at listening as you are at talking. One reason you're so good as an interviewer is that you have the invaluable knack of putting people instantly at ease. They tell you things. Even the Professor.'

Georgina's reaction blazed out of her slightly slanted topaz eyes. 'Dear Max, you're so good to me!'

'Ah, well. . . .' Max shrugged weakly. 'If you've gotta go, you've gotta go. Still, that leaves me with a big space to fill. I sure hope this brother of yours can learn to solve his own problems—and soon. The mere fact that he's called on you means he's not, even yet, independent. Tell him, Georgie, he can't always run back to mother. It's been hard enough for you keeping yourself afloat.'

'He has to have someone, Max,' Georgina offered, softly, reflectively, tolerant of her brother's bouts of neediness. 'My mother adored him. I guess he was her favourite.'

Max gave her a wry look. 'You want Richard to grow up, Georgie. *Let* him!'

CHAPTER THREE

Two days later Georgina was travelling to the Outback. The whole country was desperately in the siege of drought, and whatever fellow traveller sat next to her on the long journey, the conversation invariably came round to the state of the country, cruelly apparent from the air. It was dry, dry, *dry*. The drought had tightened its grip over the past two years, causing great economic loss and imposing severe hardship on the notoriously long-suffering people of the Inland.

'The Timeless Land,' an old-timer told her. 'The drought will break; it always does.'

Yet the plight of small farmer and great pastoralist alike was desperate, and the great herds of sheep and cattle found little to eat on the desiccated land. Even the monsoon that usually deluged the tropical North and penetrated deep into the country had failed, and the nation was still reeling from the horror of the worst bush fires in history; fire storms that overwhelmed parts of the States of Victoria and South Australia.

'Maybe the Royals will bring the rain in,' the little elderly lady who sat across the aisle from Georgina on the last leg of her flight whispered softly. Georgina smiled and nodded, and dashed away a few involuntary tears that welled. One of her colleagues had just returned from the charred ashes that were the town of Cockatoo, visibly altered by what he had seen. His reporting of human suffering, the few miracles and the abundant heroism had touched them all deeply. The rain *must* come, or the terrible heartbreak would go on.

'Looking forward to a reunion, are you?' the spry, elderly lady asked her. Georgina had noticed her boarding the plane in Brisbane, yet she still looked bandbox-fresh, in her navy silk suit and white ruffled blouse, her silvery-grey hair curling away from a sweet, alert face.

'Yes,' Georgina answered. 'I'm going out to my brother. He has two small children, and I'm longing to see them.'

'On the land, is he?'

'He's been working for almost a year on a place called Rambulara.'

'Rambulara!' the smile in the lady's eyes deepened. 'Fancy that! Why, my son-in-law would be your nearest neighbour. I'm Nell Donleavy, by the way.'

'Georgina Hamilton,' Georgina smiled.

'What a lovely name, Georgina, and it suits you. I remember noticing you in Brisbane. You have such a magnificent mane of hair—that colour! I used to have a string of amber beads just like that. Anyway, my son-in-law's property is on your north-north-west border. Nothing like so huge or important as Rambulara, but a big station all the same—Windarra. Bruce, that's my son-in-law, is great friends with Quinn—Quinn Shieffield.'

'I've never met him,' said Georgina.

'Then you've a treat in store. Wonderful man, is Quinn—and such style! I've never been in a more thrilling house in my life than the homestead. Why, coming down that staircase made me feel just like Scarlett O'Hara! People don't have houses like that any more, and small wonder. One could never get around them. But still, they're splendid to admire and the Shieffields have never been short of cash. They tell me Quinn is into mining these days?'

Georgina shook her tawny head smilingly. 'I wouldn't know.'

'Always been clever people, the Shieffields. Into everything, so they'll always have a back-up. Of course, they've known tragedy too. Quinn's brother was killed in a dreadful accident and his father, the finest horseman ever, was killed in a freak fall when they were out on muster.'

'That must have been terrible,' Georgina said feelingly.

'They say so.' The old lady's voice shook a little. 'They say Sarah, that's Quinn's mother, has become very bitter. Two terrible tragedies and in such a short time. She goes away for long periods and stays away, but she always comes back. It gets you, the Inland.'

Georgina nodded, well believing it. They continued chatting on and off until their plane began its descent, and looking out of the window Georgina thought she had never seen so much open land in her life. It was immense, primeval, the rolling plains country of the west. Either it was appallingly dry, as now, or a vast open drain of floodwaters that moved south into the legendary stronghold of the cattle kings, the Channel Country, and on towards the deserts and saltpans of the Dead Heart. That was the way of it; either a feast or a famine. Georgina had spoken to many a laconic westerner on the long journey, and it was obvious they took the good times with the bad philosophically. Fortunately most of the great sheep and cattle stations, though endlessly plagued by drought, lay in the Great Artesian Basin area, an immense geological depression where artesian and sub-artesian water could be tapped for stock and domestic use. They were right in the midst of sheep territory now, almost on the Tropic of Capricorn, but the important Outback town was a major link in the beef road-train system that transported cattle to the coast from the Channel Country stations. Here, Captain Starlight, the bush-ranger, had carried out one of the greatest and most daring stock thefts in history; a thousand head of cattle captured!

'Well, here we are safely,' Mrs Donleavy smiled at her.

'I'm quite excited!' Georgina confessed.

'So am I. I couldn't make it out for Christmas, I went to New Zealand to my daughter Meg, but I'm here at last!'

Georgina walked down the steps of the aircraft transfixed by the swimming sea of mirage and the greatest burst of heat that had ever rushed at her. It seemed so powerful it might crack her skin. Yet the sweet-faced Mrs Donleavy paced her briskly to the terminal, looking as fresh as a daisy washed clean by the dew.

'Now don't forget, you're going to visit us some time,' she said. 'Perhaps Quinn will fly you over, or Bruce will pick you up. I'm sure we could have dropped you off had we known you were coming.'

Georgina murmured something and hurried after her, certain she would be singed before she reached the shade. All Australians were used to a golden sun, but this was so brilliant, so blinding, it was savage. She would have to slather herself with moisturiser or finish up a dreary, wrinkled wreck. No wonder Jilly with her delicate English skin was looking the worse for wear!

The baggage came first, then they were walking through to the large, open lounge. 'There's my family! Come and meet them,' Mrs Donleavy said excitedly, and although Georgina didn't want to intrude she could see her new-found friend wanted her to.

She followed at a distance, seeing this fragile little lady swept off her feet by a big, sunbronzed individual who had obviously never suffered a mother-in-law problem in his life. The pretty blonde woman beside him was so like Mrs Donleavy she just had to be her daughter, Ruth.

Within moments Georgina was gathered into the family circle, warmed by the friendliness and honest good cheer that was coming her way. 'I don't know why Quinn couldn't have let me know,' Bruce Winton repeated for perhaps the fifth time. 'No trouble at all taking you home.'

'I'm not at all sure if Mr Shieffield is coming for me,' Georgina said hesitantly.

'No one else he'd trust with the Super King,' Ruth

Winton smiled. 'It's been a pleasure to meet you, Miss Hamilton. We'll be in touch.'

And then she was alone. For well over an hour. She didn't realise at the beginning, as she shook her tawny mane out and sat jauntily in the midst of her luggage, that she was raising the collective male temperature. Even in a large city she would stand out for her vital, long-legged good looks, but here in this Outback town she was very nearly a breathless sensation. Or so it would appear. Many a bright-eyed young man dressed in the traditional garb of the West, narrow jeans, bush shirt, high boots and a wide hat, gave her a long stare or an exploratory smile, and one a lot bolder than the rest sauntered over.

'Howdy!'

'Hello there.' Georgina gave him a pleasant enough smile. After all, one couldn't always judge a book by its cover.

'You look awful lonesome,' he went on.

'Not at all,' she said unconcernedly, waving her hand. 'I'm waiting for my brother.'

'Sure it's not a lover?' Tiny little sparks jetted in his eyes. 'Girls as pretty as you ought to be locked up.'

'Gosh,' she groaned, 'I thought lines like that were dead!'

'Lines?' His eyebrows twitched in shock.

'Of course, I'm not surprised. You mightn't get much practice out here.'

'I do my best, ma'am,' he drawled with a rallying of spirit. 'God knows you couldn't be anything else but a city girl, with your glossy make-up and smart clothes.'

'Heck and I thought I wasn't showing it!' grinned Georgina.

'At least can I sit down?'

'It sounds to me as if you don't need that much encouragement?' Georgina tucked her luggage all around her.

'There now,' he sat down as near as he could beside her, 'I'm beginning to feel much better. Who is your brother, by the way? Couldn't be anyone important. I know everyone around here.'

'In fact you don't,' Georgina returned blithely, 'so don't boast of it. You don't know my brother. He *is* important.'

'Oh, yeah?' the young man snorted. 'Is he a King, or a Hunter, or a Shieffield?'

'He's known Quinn Shieffield for some considerable time,' Georgina replied casually.

'Liar,' he returned unforgivably. 'I suspect you just made that up, and I know your motive.'

'Really? What?' She gave him a cool, disparaging glance.

'To frighten me off.'

'And wisely. Quinn doesn't like my being annoyed.'

'So why isn't he here?' he shot back triumphantly. 'You've been waitin' more'n an hour.'

'Perhaps he had an urgent call to make first.' Georgina flung a look over her shoulder. 'Look, if you're after a little entertainment surely there's a Space Invaders around here?'

'Hey, hey now!' He moved closer and clutched her arm. 'Why act this way, city girl? Don't you know what it is to be friendly?'

'You're far too friendly for me,' Georgina said briskly. 'Would you please take your hand off my arm.'

'Sure, Red,' he drew back with an impudent grin. 'Only you're not red, precisely, are you? More like a pretty little marmalade kitten with those long, spittin' eyes.'

'I'm not little, and I'm more like a tiger!' Georgina said dangerously. 'If you don't let go of my arm, I shall scream for assistance.'

'Gee, whatever for?' the young man gave a short, excited laugh. 'You sure are fiery!'

'Sure am.'

He let go of her hastily—too hastily, Georgina judged. His slouching spine straightened up and his cheeky brown eyes changed to total sobriety. 'Don't you dare say nuthin' about me,' he warned through his teeth. 'I'm sorry, anyway. You just brought out my protective instincts—and that's the God's truth.'

'Why, what scared you?' Georgina laughed. She swung around instantly, just in time to catch the evident, faint disgust on the face of the man who was making straight for her. Not a knight in shining armour, not a man to make one feel comfortable, but a man so blazingly arrogant and superior that there was a sudden answering blaze in her.

'Miss Hamilton?' The voice matched the appearance, and Georgina brought her hand up into position before she chanced into an involuntary curtsey.

'Why, yes, you must be Mr Shieffield?' she answered with unholy reverence. 'I can't tell you how glad I am to see you.'

'Really?' There was an expression on his face she heartily detested. 'It seems to me *you* would never find yourself cut off—not even in the middle of the Birdsville Track.'

'Handy to know if I ever find myself there.' Sparks were shooting between them, some current of man–woman antagonism. 'Everyone has been very kind.' There, that should let that little goon off the hook.

'No question.' His stunningly blue eyes looked both amused and contemptuous. She had never seen eyes quite so blue, like the heart of a flame. 'Have you much luggage?'

'Not really,' she tossed her amber hair back. 'I only expect to be here a month.'

'Then you must know something your brother doesn't.'

'Indeed no.' Blue was his colour; his shirt was the exact colour. 'I didn't realise *you'd* be coming for me, Mr Shieffield,' she said sweetly.

'And you're not particularly pleased about it either.' He lifted his hand to an attendant, who hurried over with a trolley.

'Why, I'm very grateful!' Georgina gave him the full benefit of her guileless topaz eyes.

'Sure of that?' He glanced down at her, so tall and rangy he made her feel positively doll-like instead of nearly five feet seven. 'You're very much like your brother, aren't you?' he commented.

She tried blinking to break the current. 'I know we were always taken for twins.'

'Lordy, yes.' The blue eyes slipped from her hair to her face and over the slender model-girl body dressed in cream linen pants with a yellow silk shirt. 'The terrible twins, no doubt?'

'Not totally. I couldn't spare the time.'

'So you're here for a good cause?' The trolley was loaded, so they made off.

'Don't sound as though you're not sure I'm going to come out of it alive!' she protested.

To her surprise, he laughed out loud. 'Nonsense. I hope you're going to enjoy it.'

'It will be a first anyway,' she told him. 'I've never been Outback.'

'You mean only catastrophe inspired you to join us?'

'No catastrophe,' she answered a little shortly. 'A marital spat.'

'Your view, not mine.'

It was like a procession along a red carpet. Everybody recognised him. It was, 'Good day, Mr Shieffield,' here, 'Mornin', Mr Shieffield' there. Nothing so egalitarian as, Quinn. A little airport runabout even took them to their special section.

'Thanks a lot, Bob.'

Georgina turned away and stared up at the plane, a Beechcraft Super King Air with Rambulara Station emblazoned along the fuselage in red and gold.

'All set, Mr Shieffield.' A mechanic appeared from around the other side, smiling gratefully as a bundle of notes were transferred to his hand.

'Thanks, Toby.'

'You can go out there with your guns blazing.' The mechanic looked at Georgina and winked.

'Let's hope I can too,' said Georgina. 'I've never been

in a light aircraft before and I'm wondering how I'll go.'

'Heck, you'll have fun!' the mechanic, Toby, laughed. 'No better pilot than Mr Shieffield here.'

He made her sit beside him on the flight deck, and her natural curiosity and enthusiasm for new things began to quell the butterflies in her stomach.

'To think your illustrious ancestor used to do his travelling on a horse.'

He smiled but didn't answer, waiting on clearance from the tower.

'Sure that isn't the engine pinging?' she asked.

A dry, drawling voice gave them clearance, and while Georgina braced herself, her slender hands interlocked and a snatch of a prayer running through her mind, they were lifting off the runway, then soaring like a bird up into the gold-spangled cobalt sky.

'A good trip home, Mr Shieffield,' the Outback voice said.

'Thanks Reg.'

'Thank God for that!' Georgina unpuckered her face. 'Is there anyone who doesn't know you?'

'Millions,' he answered casually, still searching the sky, 'but no one in this part of the world. That's the beautiful thing about the Outback—we all know one another.'

'Old friends.'

'That's right.' Now they were at cruising altitude he turned his head and looked at her, really *looked* at her, and Georgina very nearly trembled in reaction. He was very handsome, very macho. One of her girl friends, a connoisseur of men, would give him a ten. In fact he rated a ten plus if macho men were your choice. Georgina preferred someone sensitive to someone who made her nervous.

'You're a journalist, Miss Hamilton?' he asked suavely.

She endeavoured to look serious. 'With *Profile* magazine. Perhaps you've heard of it?'

'I've heard of it. I can't say I've bought it.'

'What a pity,' she said 'We run some very good articles.'

'What on new hair styles?'

'When you can afford one, you should buy one,' she said.

'Sorry,' he laughed. It was an intensely attractive sound. 'According to your brother you have everything—beauty, brains, personality, character.'

'You know what brothers are like.' Georgina turned her head away so he wouldn't see her flush.

'Actually,' he said, 'I've never met a jewel.'

'By our deeds you shall know us.' She tried to match his mocking tone. 'I wondered, Mr Shieffield, if while I'm out here, you'd allow me to interview you.'

'I'd rather die,' he said firmly.

'I'm perfectly serious,' she told him.

'So am I.'

He had a superb profile—wide forehead, straight nose, a beautifully sculptured mouth, excellent jawline. Even she could hardly be blamed if she gave him a ten. 'There's nothing unusual about it,' she pointed out. 'I've interviewed a good many people in the public eye.'

'Mercifully,' he said lightly, 'I'm not.'

'Perhaps we could speak of this at another time. I've brought some back issues of *Profile* with me.'

'Journalists frequently do. Especially if they have a little bit of their own to show.'

'Let's talk about Rambulara,' she suggested. 'It's safer.'

'Let's talk about your brother.' His dark, decisive voice took on a diamond edge. 'You may not realise it, Miss Hamilton, but I've been very lenient with him.'

'I'm sure you have!' For Richard's sake she had to sound conciliatory. Besides, he probably was. He looked arrogant but fair. 'I'm hoping, Mr Shieffield, you might be lenient for just a little longer. I'm sure we'll be able to work things out.'

'We?' He shot a sapphire glance at her. 'Does this mean you and me?'

'No, it means Rick and me.'

'And what about our little absent Jilly? Does she have no part in this?'

Georgina bowed her tawny head. 'Jill is at the end of her tether.'

'I'm not surprised.' His expression hardened into something grim and cynical.

'Could you explain that, if it's possible?' she begged.

'Your brother has one great redeeming feature,' he told her. 'He's immensely likeable.'

'Is that why you employed him?'

'I employed him,' he said deliberately, 'because he came to me for a job and he didn't come alone. He had a little slip of a wife and two of the cutest kids I've ever seen. I guess I hired him on the kids alone or the goodness of my heart. No way did he rate then or now as a cattleman.'

'Well, hardly,' Georgina said loyally. 'He was totally inexperienced.'

'Nothing to do with applying for the job.'

'Are you trying to tell me he's not efficient?'

'He's efficient enough,' Quinn Shieffield said dryly, 'if he'd only do what he was told. It strikes me your brother thinks all life's a game, a sort of boy's adventure. He's incredibly careless at times. I have to have a man watching him so he won't get himself killed.'

'He's still very young, you know,' Georgina said persuasively. 'Can't you just put it down to *joie de vivre*?'

'Not any longer,' he confided. 'I have to insist he gets his act together or he'll have to go.'

'But he loves it!' Georgina protested, rather pathetically.

'Sure!' He gave her a look of frank amusement. 'It's a helluva lot of fun!'

'He'll settle down.'

'Yes, but what shall we do in the meantime? What's

his wife going to do? His children? Why couldn't she have come to me instead of hitching an unauthorised ride? That's what I'm there for, to mediate where I can.'

'And it's a great policy,' Georgina said dryly.

'Don't try to butter *me* up, Miss Hamilton. You and your brother are very heavily endowed in that department. I feel very sorry for your sister-in-law.'

'So do I.'

He glanced at her curiously. 'Do you know, your brother talks about you all the time? I'll be damned if he doesn't do it in front of his own wife!'

'But that's reasonable,' said Georgina. 'Our parents were killed when Rick was only fifteen. It was a terrible experience, and I had to sort of become mother.'

'He told me how it started.'

'*What* started?' She sent him a sparkling, topaz look.

'This rather obsessive bond.'

'Rubbish!' she protested.

'Your brother told me he needed to get away to make a life of his own and allow you to make yours. He realised he was relying on you too heavily for support.'

'Maybe because I'm family,' Georgina said fierily. 'Don't your family rely on you?'

'They certainly do.' His blue eyes went over her in an encompassing wave. 'In the first place because I'm head of the family and in the second place because I'm a man. A man doesn't pressure his womenfolk no matter what. He doesn't burden them with his failures and frustrations. As *I* see it, the man is the guardian figure. He may need a woman's love and support, but he can't lean on her. She's too vulnerable. The only way your brother's marriage is going to work for both of them is for him to accept the guardian role. As it is, your sister-in-law has to struggle too hard. She can't live up to your radiant image. Possibly that's always going to be too tall an order, given that early dependency, and she can't compete with an immature husband's mad enthusiasms. He's utterly rebellious at the real idea of marriage, you know. For that matter, both of them are so young.'

'Yes.' Georgina was still smarting over his charge of obsessive, emotional attachments. 'I dare say only in the best of circumstances can one hang off until the thirties.'

'I gather that's a shot at me?'

'Not at all,' she said innocently. 'I can see you're a man of real weight.'

'Thank you,' he gave her a jeering smile. 'And how come an exotic creature like you isn't married?'

'The fact is,' she said easily, 'I'm as serious-minded as you.'

'You don't look it. You look every bit as extravagant as your brother said.'

'What does extravagant mean, exactly?' Rightly or wrongly this man was disturbing her greatly. There was even a hard, tight knot in her chest.

'Made up of all sorts of energy. Bright, flashing colour. Young women like you, Miss Hamilton, could never go unnoticed.'

'Well, I don't think anyone ever said orange is a comfortable colour.'

'It's quite lovely linked to creamy skin and golden eyes,' said Quinn Shieffield.

'Thank you.' Far from being pleased she felt like an unwilling moth being singed by a flame. 'May I take you into my confidence, Mr Shieffield?' she asked presently.

'Oh, please do.'

She couldn't imagine what was amusing him, but something was. She dipped her head and bit her lip.

'Come on, what's the matter?' he urged.

'You must keep this all to yourself.'

'Torturers couldn't force it out of me though they tried a hundred times!' Quinn Shieffield grinned.

'I'm serious.' She suddenly went pale.

'You're sick of coping. Is that it? You'll have to tell your brother sooner or later. All good relationships are a two-way thing. He has to quit relying on you, as you very well know.'

'I can't abandon him, Mr Shieffield,' she said a little self-righteously.

'Why not? Let him deal with his own affairs.'

'Someone has to look after the children,' she pointed out. 'How *are* they?'

'Missing their mother, of course. But apart from that, they're being very well looked after. Our housekeeper, Janet, happens to be very fond of them, so they're not missing meals and we have an excellent little house girl, Lulah, to look after them.'

'Rick didn't tell me.' Her eyes were on him, a little frown between her delicate, naturally dark brows.

'You bet he didn't. Rick likes the idea of shouldering everything himself, but unfortunately ideas aren't deeds. I expect he was doted on from the cradle.'

'Mummy loved him. Idolised him,' Georgina said sadly. 'And who could blame her? He was just the sweetest little boy in the world.'

'I can't think he was any sweeter than you.'

'Oh yes, he was.' Georgina lifted her eyes. 'I was the one for lively pranks. Some of them were even disastrous.'

'And then it all came to an end.'

'Yes—one dreadful day.'

'Poor Georgina! It's impossible, isn't it, to totally dissolve pain?'

'You must know.' A small jagged sigh emerged with the words. 'Even being the heir to a mighty cattle empire can't protect one from terrible tragedy.'

'No.' The single word was toneless, yet it made a lot of power behind it. 'Yet you're a survivor, aren't you? You've tried hard.'

'There was no other choice,' she shrugged. 'Life goes on. I had Rick to worry about.'

'And you're still worrying?'

'Jill has come to me,' she admitted, sounding spent.

'I thought she might. The way she used to say, "Georgie" I thought you were *her* sister, at first.'

'We're very fond of one another,' said Georgina.

'Anyway, this is in strict confidence. I don't intend to tell Rick. . . .'

'You'll *have* to.'

'I won't.' Her delicately determined jaw firmed. 'Let him suffer a while.'

'Are you sure he *is* suffering?' Quinn Shieffield asked dryly. 'He's by no means convinced his wife has up and left him. He thinks she's flown off in a fit of the sulks.'

'But she's distraught, desperate!' Georgina protested. It was absolutely impossible to tell him why.

'Your brother thinks all women are difficult. Except you. Jill has flown off in a tantrum, and he's going to retaliate by ignoring her. I think he figures she'll come home when she uses up all her money.'

'But she hasn't *got* any. Or very little.'

'Apparently their little piggy-bank is gone,' Quinn told her.

'Jill said nothing about that. Probably she's just hidden it.'

'You're joking!' His blue eyes were very sceptical.

'And I think that's very cynical of you. Jilly wouldn't spend their savings.'

'Perhaps not totally, no. I do have some knowledge of women, Miss Hamilton.'

'Please call me Georgina,' she said charmingly. 'I know I'll never be free to call you Quinn.'

'Why not?'

'Think of it,' she said. 'I have to acknowledge your position.'

'The only sensible thing to do.' He tilted his head back a little, the very picture of male splendour. 'Mr Shieffield it is, then. Missy, as it happens, calls me Quinn very sweetly. But then she's only a baby.'

'And what am I, anyway?' Georgina exclaimed suddenly.

'Very different, Miss Hamilton. That's for sure.'

CHAPTER FOUR

RICK was there to meet them. And the children.

'Missy darling!' Georgina went down on her knees to grasp the little girl who rushed towards her. 'My sweet girl!' She covered a moist, hot little face with kisses.

'Aunty!' Timmy's voice sang. 'You're *here*! Daddy told us you'd come.'

'Okay, so you've grown!' She never meant to, but the happy tears slid down her face.

'Georgie!' While the children hugged her Richard took his sister's face in his hands and kissed her nose. 'It's great to see you.'

'Oh, Rick—a *beard*?' Georgina exclaimed.

'Yes, doesn't it look good?' Rick had indeed grown a curly beard and his golden eyes glowed. 'I can't thank you enough, Mr Shieffield, for bringing her.'

Quinn Shieffield merely nodded, regarding the loving tableau with half cynical, half kindly eyes. 'You look a very well integrated family, except that you require one vital person.'

'Who told me to go to hell,' Rick hissed in his sister's ear.

'That will be taken care of,' she assured Quinn Shieffield soberly.

'I was waiting to hear from your brother.'

'Just like Georgie said, sir.'

Quinn Shieffield ran a hand through his crisp raven-black hair. 'That sounded like an echo.'

Rick scarcely heard, still accustoming himself to the sight of his sister's face. 'Don't you think she's just as I described her?' he turned questioningly to his boss.

'Oh, shut up, Rick,' Georgina begged.

'Both of you would have delighted someone like

40

Michelangelo,' he returned dryly. 'You're pure sculpture.'

'I love you, Aunty,' Melissa said against her neck.

'And I really love you, darling.'

'Aah!' Melissa drew a shallow, shuddery breath and began to sob. 'Where's Mummy?'

'You know where she is, darling. She's having a lovely holiday.'

'*Is* she?' Timmy looked up at her with familiar, topaz eyes.

'Of course she is, Timmy. That's why I'm here—so Mummy can have a holiday.'

'Mummy!' Melissa wailed, relaxing her full weight in Georgina's slender arms.

'I expect she'd like a ride on my shoulder,' Quinn Shieffield said unexpectedly. He came to them and put his arms around Melissa's adorably compact, surprisingly heavy small body. 'Up we go, Bubbles.'

'Because of her curls.' Timmy looked up at his aunt and grinned. 'Can't I cut mine off?'

'We just can't seem to solve the matter of these curls,' said Georgina. Both of the children had inherited long familiar curly haloes. 'Perhaps a little trim.'

'Daddy needs the trim,' said Timmy.'

'Oooh!' Melissa's sobs were miraculously checked. 'Funny, Quinn,' she cried, peering down into Quinn Shieffield's devastating face.

'See, she calls him Quinn,' Timmy told his aunt in a voice that was supposed to be shocked but sounded admiring. 'She's too small to know any better. I dare not call Mr Shieffield that.'

'Why not?' Georgina wanted what his answer would tell her. 'Gosh, Aunty, he's the Boss. He's the man who owns a *million* acres.'

'By crikey!' Georgina mocked, yet she could scarcely believe she was here in a whole new world.

They all piled into the waiting jeep, the men in the front, Quinn Shieffield driving, and Georgina in the back her two arms around the children while they lay against her, their soft, silky faces flushed with happiness and excitement. Melissa, in fact, was giggling helplessly and showing no signs of stopping, and Georgina put it down to a reaction from anxiety. She had never been without her sweet, gentle mother. Timmy, for his part, kept lifting his aunt's hand and kissing it, and Georgina was pierced through with love—and a painful anger. Couldn't Rick see what he was risking? He wasn't the first man to be dazed by another woman's attractions, but he had promised to love and honour his wife. God knows, that was what marriage was supposed to be all about—love and honour; a lifetime commitment. One had to hold to a marriage tightly, as one held to a loved child. It was clear that this Lucinda Shieffield was only using Rick for her own amusement, exercising her power. What kind of exchange was that?

'Missy will be sick if she keeps on giggling,' Timmy whispered.

'Won't.' Melissa shook her head, and roared with laughter.

'Please don't, darling,' said Georgina. 'I want you to see your presents.'

Melissa exchanged her giggles for hugs, and Georgina looked about her with dreamy, captured eyes. Here, the terrible realities of drought seemed far away. What they were passing through was for all the world like a model settlement with lots of buildings, large and small, all apparently freshly painted and gleaming white through the tall stands of gums.

'That's Mr Donovan's place!' Timmy announced with a look of pleasure. 'He's Mr Shieffield's overseer. He has a big red beard. You'll like him.'

'I will?' Georgina looked out at the grandest of several very picturesque, colonial bungalows, low-set structures surrounded by verandahs and their own small garden. They looked very attractive and they said a lot for the accommodation of Shieffield employees.

'I can't get over how you've grown, Timmy,' she smiled. 'I just can't!'

'Daddy said you'd notice. And I'd better tell you, we have a dog.'

'Oh, lovely. What kind?'

'A dingo.'

'A *what*?' Georgina held her flying mane back with one hand.

'Daddy brought him back when he was only a little puppy,' Timmy told her. 'He's as tame as anything.'

'I assume Daddy has checked this out?'

'He's just the same as any other dog. He loves us.'

'Great. I just hope he's going to like me.'

They pulled up in front of a bungalow that Georgina found intensely charming. A sweeping roof, painted green, covered the deep verandahs closed in a wooden bracketing and the white timber columns supported a prolifically blossoming Virginia creeper. There were two sets of shuttered, dormer windows on either side of the front door and the front door itself had little panels of stained glass. It occurred to Georgina that a charming little colonial like this would be much sought after in the city.

'How pleasant!' she said.

'Quinn's house,' Melissa informed her, 'is a *castle*.'

'It has gold paintings on the wall,' Timmy added.

'I can well imagine,' Georgina said dryly, 'and I've only seen it from the air.' Rambulara homestead had indeed looked imposing, a massive structure as befitting a monument to the Shieffield family. From the air it had dominated its satellite town, but it was impossible to see it now. Georgina guessed it would be perhaps a mile away. She could see no sign of the huge ornamental lake the main house overlooked.

'I'll speak to you alone for a moment, Richard,' Quinn Shieffield said deliberately as Richard set the luggage down on the verandah.

'Yes, sir.'

Georgina, with one child in her arms and the other grasping the pocket of her linen slacks, came to the verandah rail. 'I did try to thank you before, but you wouldn't let me,' she said.

'No trouble at all, Miss Hamilton,' he looked up at her. 'If there's anything you need, just check with the station store.'

'May I wander around?' she asked.

'Of course. Your arrival has been something of a topic of conversation, so everyone will know who you are even if you didn't look your brother's twin. When you settle in, I'd like you to join us for dinner at the house. Perhaps tomorrow?'

'But the children—?' She looked down at Timmy's glossy red-brown head.

'They have their father, in case you've forgotten.'

'Sure!' Richard called out to reassure her. For an exalted moment there he had thought he too had been invited—something quite extraordinary in his situation.

'See you!' Quinn Shieffield sketched a salute to which Georgina and the children responded with a spontaneous wave, then he clapped his hand on Richard's shoulder and all but propelled him back towards the jeep.

'Is Daddy getting into trouble?' Timmy asked almost fearfully.

'Good heavens, no!' Georgina answered him, thinking the same thing. 'Mr Shieffield is just giving him some instructions.'

'The Boss is very good to us. Just remember that, Mummy said.'

The 'Mummy' was enough to make Melissa's face crumple, so Georgina turned about calmly, demanding to be introduced to their dog. 'What's his name?' she waved a finger in front of Melissa's uncertain face.

'Tiger!' Melissa gave a huge chuckle.

'Tiger? Isn't that a little frightening?'

'He'd have to be much bigger, Aunty,' Timmy reassured her. 'Anyway, Tiger doesn't like scaring people.'

'The saints be praised.' She looked back towards the men, but they were still deep in conversation. Or rather

Quinn Shieffield, she guessed, was laying down the law. There was a decidedly formidable set to his stance and expression. 'Do you know what I'd like now?' she said, and looked down at the children.

'No, Aunty, *what?*'

'A nice cup of tea.'

It wasn't until after dinner that night that Georgina felt free to conduct a serious conversation with her brother. The children were in bed, finally, and Tiger, a handsome dog, little more than a puppy, settled in the little closed-in annexe at the rear of the house. Jilly had hung it with a variety of ferns and other plants and it looked very pretty and cool. When Tiger was a little older and less interested in almost anything as food 'Mummy' was going to put a lot of her favourite plants on the ground.

Richard was warned of his sister's thoughts as her vivid face grew sombre.

'Don't be angry with me, Georgie,' he sighed.

'We have to talk, Rick,' she told him firmly.

'I know.' Richard got up from the kitchen table and began to pace the room. 'Jill's with you, isn't she?'

'No, I'm here.'

'I mean, she's at home.'

'I don't know where she is,' said Georgina.

'Don't be stupid, Georgie. I knew she'd go to you.'

'So who else *could* she go to?' Georgina started out fierily, then hastily remembering the children, lowered her voice. 'She has no one, absolutely no one, but you and me.'

'Well, don't blame me because she scooted,' Richard said. 'She's so much a child, marriage is too much for her.'

'And what about you?' Georgina's eyes were very clear and direct. 'Come back here and sit down. All this pacing, Rick, is a kind of running away.'

'I love her, Georgie, you know I do.'

'No, I *don't* know, Rick—and take that silly, pious

look off your face. How can you hurt someone you love?'

'Easily. God knows you've hurt my feelings plenty of times, but I realised you were always doing your best for me.'

'Thank goodness for that!' Georgina resisted the impulse to do it one more time. 'The thing is, Rick, we're brother and sister. Brothers and sisters can fight forever and always be friends. By contrast with blood a lot of other relationships are pretty frail. We accept one another, whatever. I know you. You know me. There's no point in either of us trying to lie to each other. I *must* know. Do you still love Jilly? If you could go back and start again, would it be Jill?'

'I can't go back and start again. That's the point.'

'Oh, God, Rick!' Georgina put out her hand and grasped her brother's. 'What are you saying?'

'I love Jilly,' he shook his head, the light dancing in the richness of his hair. 'But she's never been wildly desirable. She's just Jilly, warm and sweet and loving, or so she was.'

'And who the hell's wildly desirable?' she charged him. 'Lucinda Shieffield?'

Rick looked up and smiled at her crazily. 'Yes.'

'Rick, you fool!' Georgina threw her brother's hand away.

'I know that,' he said. 'I know she's not interested in me.'

'You like it here, don't you, Rick?'

'I love it,' he agreed readily. 'I don't think I could ever go back to the city again.'

'You'll lose your job here.'

'Why?' Rick looked at her with an expression of unspeakable fright. 'Mr Shieffield didn't say anything to you, did he?'

'No,' Georgina said mechanically. 'He can't be aware of your . . . interest in his sister-in-law. Not yet. That's why you've got to end it.'

'End what?' Rick suddenly pounded the table with

his fist. 'There's nothing to end. A couple of rides, a few conversations. She's a very unhappy woman.'

'Granted she has reason to be, as she lost her husband,' Georgina agreed.

'She didn't love him.'

'It didn't deter her any from marrying him?'

'That was on the rebound,' Rick said, drawing circles on the tablecloth. 'Quinn was cruel to her.'

'He doesn't look a cruel man to me,' she said firmly.

'No, he's a great guy, but love can do funny things to a man.'

'You can say that again!' Georgina muttered with disgust. 'It can make a man forget little things, like a wife and kids. And don't forget to fling in a job.'

'She loves him, you know,' Rick said with difficulty. 'Whatever he did to her, she still loves him.'

'So leave them alone, Rick. God, you have no place in their world! Have you ever stopped to think that a woman like that couldn't do without the things she's used to? Have you ever made love to her?'

The question seemed to daze Richard. 'She let me kiss her once.'

'Did she, the skunk!'

'God, Georgie, you've no idea!' he protested.

'Good, was it?'

'Like nothing I've ever known. Burning, devouring.'

'Oh, hell!' Georgina felt the cold breath of fear on her neck. This woman, Lucinda Shieffield, projected magic, albeit black. Richard's feeling for her was probably all illusion, but while she looked on him it held him in her grip.

'You've never been in love have you, Georgie?' Rick said, watching her. She was sitting with her arms spread out on the table and her head bowed like a woman in supplication.

'Sure I have.' She brought up her head, her eyes like jewels in the bright light. 'I was madly in love with one of my lecturers for about six months. Then I was rather fond of Michael . . .'

'So you'll never understand.'

'Why not, for God's sake? I'm a grown woman. I've never been short of an admirer . . .'

'Too many, in fact.'

'I know what it's like to be temporarily dazzled.' For the life of her she couldn't tell him her reaction to Quinn Shieffield. 'How can you love someone if you don't like and admire them?'

'Never mind.' Richard turned his handsome mouth down and looked away wryly.

'I understand, Rick—I *do*. Probably she's very beautiful.'

'Wait until you see her,' he said, and there was distress in his eyes. 'She's your direct opposite. Where you're open and warm and friendly, she's cold and secretive. Where you're bright and glowing, she's a study in black and white. The first time I saw her I couldn't tear my eyes away from her.'

'Oh, poor Jilly!' Georgina groaned. 'Have you entirely forgotten the girl you married? The girl you *insisted* on marrying; no matter how much I begged you both to wait a little. You're Jilly's whole world. She's even left her children because she can't take this infatuation. She's suffering, Rick, believe me.'

'Good.' Rick's eyes were strangely bright. 'All right, so I'm infatuated! I have absolutely no intention of leaving my wife. The situation will never arise. Lucinda enjoys my adoration. She has no feeling for me—I tell you she's insane about her own brother-in-law. So much so that it's rather terrible to see. And he *is* cruel to her—I've heard him. You can hardly suppose I'm making it up. They have a different way of talking from us. We crackle and burn; theirs is some terrible cold war. Sometimes I think he hates her, but the more he cuts her down the more punishment she seems to ask for.'

'What a dreadful existence,' Georgina said. 'Perhaps he blames her for his brother's death, who knows? But there's no need for her to stay here. I'm told her people

are very rich, and I'm sure her poor husband left her
well provided for.'

'She won't let Quinn go.' Rick's vibrant voice had
dropped to a whisper. 'Oh, God, Georgie, I'm sorry. I
know Jill is worth a hundred of Lucinda. When we
came here we were never happier in our lives. The place
is so magnificent—the peace and the freedom, and
Quinn is such a great boss. Then Lucinda seemed to go
out of her way to get me alone. I was amazed when she
started chatting to me. She speaks to no one but the
household; everyone else she just treats like dirt. She
used to make me furious, the way she just ignored Jilly.
Poor little Jilly, with despair in her eyes. Who could be
nasty to Jilly?'

'*You*,' Georgina pointed out emphatically. 'You're
waffling on about some sinister obsession for a woman
who's only using you, God knows for what purpose.
Probably to sow discontent in Quinn Shieffield's savage
heart. That's all there is to it, Rick. She's a beautiful
woman with a lot of experience and she's using her
power to wreck a marriage. Not because she's in love
with you—oh, no; I might have some compassion for
her if I thought that. But she sounds as if she just craves
excitement. She doesn't care that she could destroy a
marriage. You said yourself she treats everyone like
dirt. People like that only have one view in life—taking
everything they want. Especially when people are idiotic
enough to give it to them without a fight.'

'You don't think I'm fighting?' Rick asked bitterly.
He stabbed his hand through his curly mop and
Georgina could see his fingers trembling. 'I don't *want*
to think of her, Georgie.'

'Oh, dear!' Georgina stared at him in horror. 'This
can't happen, Rick,' she said. 'I'm here to help you fight
temptation.'

'That's my girl!' Richard took a deep breath and
laughed. 'Remember that time you had to go up and see
the Headmaster?'

'Yes. He looked stunned when he saw me. He

thought me too young for such a big responsibility, but he was very kind and understanding. You can't go on expecting leniency all your life, Rick. I can't go on pleading your case. I'd like to, because I love you, but I can't. It's no good for *you*. You have to take hold of your own life. You should have gone after Jilly and brought her back.'

'Not after the things she said to me,' Rick said resentfully. 'I'll tell you, she left me feeling I might as well be hanged for a sheep as a lamb.'

'She accused you of having an affair with Mrs Shieffield?'

'She accused me of the lot!' Richard stood up with an expression of male outrage on his face. 'In fact she screeched until she was breathless and the kids were screaming. How's that for a responsible little mother? She didn't even know the kids were there. I didn't even know she was that kind of person, screeching and screeching like a fishwife—a lot of rubbish about what I'd taken from her. And I said nothing, except to tell her she was hysterical with jealousy and she was letting herself go.'

'Oh, poor Jilly!' Georgina moaned. 'Did you have to say that?'

'Well, she is,' Richard protested. 'She used to have a lovely figure, now she's downright plump, and that's a simple fact. When I first told her tactfully that she was putting on a bit of weight, did she go on a diet? She did not. She started making cakes—exotic ones with tons of chocolate curls. She's a good cook too, but I can ride it off. I never put on weight anyway. Jilly's just packed it on and nothing can stop her. It's a revelation to see a girl lose her looks.'

'She hasn't lost her looks at all,' protested Georgina. 'I guarantee she can lose that weight in a month, probably less. Her eating, Rick, is very understandable. Food gives satisfaction, and she wasn't getting any from you.'

'Too right she was,' Richard agreed. 'That's what

made it so hard to see what all the wailing was about. I wasn't unfaithful to her. Given the chance, I don't think I would be. I'm not a rotter who forgets he has a wife as soon as she's out of sight. I didn't kiss Lucinda—I'll swear somehow she got me to kiss her. None of it's clear, even now. I can only remember my whole body shaking and feeling sick at the same time. I don't want trouble, Georgie. I've had enough of that.'

'Yet it seems to follow you around.' Georgina looked at him with agonisingly clear eyes. In his time in the Outback Rick had become leaner, harder, more powerful-looking. He was undoubtedly a splendid-looking young man even with that ridiculous beard. His shoulders were broad, tapering to a small waist and lean flanks. He even looked taller, well over six feet. She had a vivid picture of the young Jilly laughing, calling him her 'archangel'. Well, the archangel, if he hadn't fallen, was teetering on the brink!

'Do you want to save your marriage, Rick? Tell me!' she urged.

He spun around with golden fire in his eyes. 'I have never for one minute even considered leaving Jill. She's the one who left *me*. I can't deny Lucinda's pull, but I'm not such a fool that I don't know she's only playing some little game, probably to keep her from feeling bored. If she was trying to make the Boss jealous, then she's going a funny way about it. When he's around, she doesn't even look my way. I'm just one of the rabble, someone you couldn't possibly know socially. There's a huge gap between the Boss and the employees around here. I guess it's a throwback to the days when they were the absolute law—still are, in a way. Lucinda Shieffield has no thought of luring me away. Her first love, her only love, was never her husband.'

'Poor man!'

'I believe it,' said Rick. 'A woman like Lucinda could make a man's life a desolation.'

'Well, that says it, doesn't it?' Georgina spoke more

calmly. 'You were right in your permanent choice. Jilly
is a good, sweet girl, mother of your children. I guess
every marriage could be haunted by a spectre some time
or other. At the end of a month, Rick, I have to go
back home. By that time Jill will have had a holiday
and achieved her old serenity. Screeching at a man
doesn't have anything to do with loving him. Your . . .
interest in Mrs Shieffield was hurting her so much. How
would you feel if Jilly developed a mad crush on, say,
Quinn Shieffield?'

'He wouldn't look at her,' said Rick. 'She's married.'

'If he *did*?'

'Oh, hell, Georgie, it couldn't happen. Jilly isn't
Quinn Shieffield's kind of person.'

'Any more than you're Lucinda's?'

'Exactly.'

'Then we'll let it drop. Believe me, kid, we're halfway
home!'

Georgina, never in her life, had begun her day at first
light. To make it worse, she had slept badly, awakened
in the early hours by a terrible howling sound unlike
anything she had ever heard before. In her confused
state she thought she was in the middle of a nightmare
peopled with monsters and werewolves. Later on she
learned that it was only Tiger indicating that he wanted
to be let out. It was a matter of interest anyway.
Dingoes had to have the eeriest howl in the whole
canine repertoire.

Richard was already in the kitchen when she
staggered in. 'You don't have to get up for me, pal,' he
said considerately and with a hypocrisy that didn't
escape her. 'How did you sleep?'

'Soundly for about half an hour or so. How come the
mastiff is silent?'

'Damned little nuisance is playing with a plastic
bottle. I suppose he's still a puppy.'

'Here, I'll do that.' Georgina took the bowl of eggs as
she was meant to. 'What will it be, the usual?'

Richard sat back happily. 'Yes, only more. Being a station hand is hard work.'

She looked at him and nodded. 'It's made you very fit.' She broke eggs into the frying pan with expert negligence. 'What's on the agenda today, pardner?'

'Well, I won't be twiddling my thumbs, that's for sure. We're shifting a mob this morning, fences this afternoon. Some of the stock were agisted to the Shieffield run in the Territory, otherwise we're managing. This is a very progressive station—the best. The Boss looks ahead to the bad times by planning in the good. He's heavily into soil conservation, that kind of thing—has scientists out, and the lot. Anyway, the advice works. We're much better off than most. We have plenty of bore water and permanent water as well. Still, we're all sweating on the rain. It's a miracle out here. The land responds like magic. One shower and all the dormant seeds spring to life and flower. It's really incredible—instant gardens!'

They talked happily through breakfast and made plans for the weekend when Rick had his time off. They had always been the most amicable conversationalists, and now Rick had lost his driven expression and was acting in many ways like a man who had just seen his beloved wife off on a well deserved holiday, with his dearest family confidante to turn to. It seemed frivolously irresponsible, but it was Rick.

' 'Morning, Aunty. Hello, Daddy.' Tim in his pyjamas moved towards them, still half suspended in sleep.

'Good morning, darling.' Georgina put her arm around him and hugged him. It was just like having her adored little brother back. 'It's a bit early to be up, isn't it?'

'I heard your voices, and for a minute I thought Mummy was back,' Timmy explained.

'No, poppet. Just me paying a visit while Mummy has a little holiday and does some shopping—most probably for *you*,' she smiled.

'Do you think so?' Timmy looked at her, half bewildered, half delighted.

'I don't want to spoil any surprises,' she told him. 'Now, seeing you're up, what would you like me to get you?'

'Let me see,' Timmy pulled himself up on to a seat. 'What did Daddy have?'

'That's it, have a hearty breakfast,' said Rick, and got up. 'You look after your aunt now, Timmy.' He ruffled his son's head.

'Yes, I will, Daddy,' said Timmy, most seriously. 'I'll show her how to climb trees.'

In fact both the children showed her around the compound, each trying to outshine the other, all of them largely enjoying themselves. This morning it was almost a ghost town, because all the men were out and there were no women on the staff.

'That's Billy,' Tim said, when an old aboriginal waved to them. 'He tells the most super stories, all about the Dreamtime. How the Great Spirit ancestors created all the animals and plants. Do you know, in a deep hole right at the top of Ayers Rock, *Oolera*, Billy calls it, don't you think it's a better name, the great Rainbow Snake lives. When he's disturbed by the rain he rears up into the sky.'

'Goodness!' Georgina confessed her amazement. 'While I'm out here I'm determined to see Ayers Rock—I mean, Oolera. I thought it was Uluru.'

'Ask Billy,' said Timmy. 'The Olgas are called Katajuta. Isn't that a lovely name? I can't really say it like Billy.'

'K'juta!' piped Melissa.

'In the olden times Billy's people used to go there for their cer . . . cer . . .'

'Ceremonies?'

'Yes, their corroborees. We've seen a corroboree,' Timmy announced proudly. 'Missy went to sleep, but I stayed awake till the end. Billy was in it. He played the didgeridoo.'

'I must persuade him to play it for me,' Georgina continued to wave. Billy sounded a kindly old fellow and she had always had a compassionate feeling for the original inhabitants of this ancient land, displaced as they were by the white man. The aboriginal culture had survived for forty thousand years, and Georgina knew she would find Billy's stories every bit as fascinating as Timmy obviously did.

'Mr Shieffield said he'd take us to Alice Springs to greet Bonnie Prince Charlie and his bride.'

'Did he *really*?'

'An' P'wince William,' Melissa smiled knowingly.

'But how lovely,' Georgina said. She had thought it might be difficult to get to Alice Springs, now it looked as if she might be able to hitch a ride with Baron Shieffield. 'When did he say this?' she questioned Timmy.

'I heard him tell Mummy. Mummy was born in England, you know, not here. Mr Shieffield understood we would love to go. Mummy had tears in her eyes. Mr Shieffield is simply the best boss in the world.'

'Sounds like it,' Georgina agreed.

As they drew near to him, Billy became more and more absorbed in his sweeping, but Timmy ran to him and pulled at his shirt sleeve. 'This is Aunt Georgie, Billy. Come and say hello.'

The old aboriginal looked up, and as he did so encountered Georgina's entrancing smile. 'Good morning, miss,' he said in what Georgina considered a very cultured tone.

'Good morning,' she said, not liking to address him by the familiar 'Billy'. Probably he was a very important person in his own tribe. He certainly had an air of strength and dignity, and snow-white hair against a dark chocolate skin. 'The children have been telling me about your wonderful stories.'

'Legends of our people.' Very gently he touched Melissa's curls with a gnarled hand. 'To make them see how it was, how it happened.'

'I would love to hear your legends some time, if you'd be kind enough to tell me,' Georgina said on a comfortable yet serious note. 'I write—I'm a journalist. Of course I'm here to look after the children while my sister-in-law is away, but I'd love to write my impressions of this ancient land, of its people. I'd be very glad to convey your feelings if you choose to speak to me.'

Billy was now looking at her straightly. 'My people don't live as they used to,' he reminded her.

'I know.'

'My people who live here are fortunate. Byamee is a great man—we can trust him, be faithful. He knows our world. He knows the land as we know it, its moods and secrets. I have been his guide and teacher on many occasions. I took his father walkabout. I attended his grandfather from my early youth.'

'Then you would know almost the whole history of Rambulara?'

'And before.' Although his eyes were thickly encased in wrinkles, the old man's regard was piercing. 'You know what Rambulara means?' He gave to the place name the most musical lilt, so much so that Georgina tried it silently on her tongue. 'Magic rainbow.'

'Really?' She lifted her eyes to the peacock sky. 'How lovely! A portent?'

'For my people. For the white master who respects this land.'

Tiger, on a lead, wanted to get up and go, but Billy turned and spoke commandingly in a soft dialect that the dingo evidently understood. It sat down again on its haunches, ears pricked. The dingo was the traditional friend of aboriginal man. The Dingo-Man was a deity, and aboriginal mythology going back many thousands of years contained story after story of the legendary wild dog. It was thought their lineage was so ancient it went back beyond the Sulukis, the hunting dogs of the Sumerians or the Afghan hounds from the Valley of the Nile.

Afterwards Billy walked with them, a comforting presence in the children's lives, but some little distance from the bungalow, he suddenly stopped and turned away. 'Good day, miss.'

'Thank you, Billy.' For a moment she forgot and called him by his name. He had been right in the middle of a story about Bunjil, the Great Eagle Hawk, so it was a little disconcerting to have him break off. 'You have a visitor, miss.'

'Oh—have I?' Georgina looked intently, but could see no one.'

'I can't see anyone at all, Billy,' said Tim.

'She has gone into the house.'

Georgina stared at him. 'Who do you mean?'

But there was nothing more Billy would say. His exit was resolute and swift.

'Well, if that isn't the darnedest thing!' Georgina muttered, and even Tiger barked, his beautiful coat standing up. Either Billy had seen a ghost or he didn't want the ghost to see him.

CHAPTER FIVE

FOR a heart-stopping moment Georgina thought she was looking at the living model for every illustration of a faerie enchantress she had ever seen.

Lucinda Shieffield was incredibly beautiful, but in a peculiarly malevolent way. Her long, centre-parted hair fell in a dead straight jet-black wave, her skin was almost deathly white, her delicate features so fine they were wondrously sharp, her eyes large, brilliant, black gem-stones, strangely opaque, hypnotic in their intensity, the nails of her uplifted hand (a curse or a spell) so long and pointed they could conceivably tear a mortal's heart out.

Melissa began to cry and Timmy clutched his aunt's hand hard.

'My poor Richard!' Georgina thought fearfully. Small wonder he had felt her wild dark excitement. Georgina could feel it herself. Without saying a word Lucinda Shieffield possessed the kind of power to strike fear into a woman and capture and enrapture every unwary male.

'You must be Georgina,' she said in a voice as mesmeric as her appearance. It wasn't a bright, clear voice like Georgina's, but a curiously harsh, soft contralto, a seeming contradiction.

'Mrs Shieffield.' For the life of her Georgina couldn't go forward, she merely inclined her head.

'*Must* you cry, little one?' Lucinda fixed her black eyes on Melissa's rosy face.

'You frightened her,' Timmy said belligerently. 'You frightened us all.'

'*Please*, Timmy!' Georgina looked down at her small nephew warningly. Ordinarily she would have corrected him further, but she was feeling Timmy's belligerence herself. Surely Lucinda had no right to open doors and undertake an inspection of an employee's bungalow? And that was what she had been doing. It rather shocked Georgina, who would have found it impossible to invade another's privacy, let alone their house. 'Is there something you particularly wanted, Mrs Shieffield?' she asked pleasantly, but making her surprise plain.

'But of course,' Lucinda gave a funny, scornful little smile, 'to meet you. You're very beautiful.'

It was said simply, as a judgment, with no shade of pleasure or admiration.

'Thank you.' Georgina picked up Melissa and held her. 'May I say the same of you?'

'Yes.' There was no way Lucinda could disbelieve it. 'I daresay the absolute contrast is a little too picturesque.'

The necessity of carrying on the usual social pleasantries seemed appalling, but what else could Georgina do? Order her out? 'Won't you sit down,' she said instead. 'May I offer you something, tea or coffee?'

'Coffee would be fine.' Lucinda gave another of her funny little smiles and turned to the suddenly tongue-tied Timmy. 'You don't like me, do you?'

Timmy unexpectedly found diplomacy. He didn't answer.

'I've had very little to do with children,' she explained to Georgina.

Did one really have to have daily contact with children to like them? Georgina wondered. Lucinda in no sense appeared a maternal woman and in fact there were many that weren't.

'I won't be a moment,' she said calmly. 'I'll just settle the children and Tiger.'

'You shouldn't have that dog,' Lucinda distinctly frowned. Like her smile, it was done with a peculiar intensity.

'Why not?' Timmy broke his enforced silence abruptly.

'It's a dingo, that's why,' Lucinda replied, making it sound like some kind of ravening monster. 'They're killers. They kill hundreds of lambs each year and they hunt in packs to cut out the calves. I'm astounded Mr Shieffield has allowed you to keep him.'

'He seems a very ordinary, friendly little dog to me,' Georgina intervened, 'but then, admittedly, I don't know much about dingoes. Anyway, he's not a pure-bred dog, he's a cross-breed. If I didn't know better, I'd say it was a collie.'

'We've tamed him,' Timmy interrupted, the nostrils of his little nose flaring. 'Billy says the dingo is the best dog on earth.'

'*Billy!*' Lucinda stared blackly at him. It was rather alarming, her stare. 'That old man?'

'Come along, children,' Georgina intervened smoothly. It was obvious Timmy had inherited the Hamilton quick temper. 'Tiger,' she called to the dog who was listening intently from the verandah, 'round the back!'

'See how intelligent he is,' Timmy couldn't resist announcing as Tiger sprang up immediately and tore around to the annexe. 'What kind of wild dog does what he's told?'

In the kitchen Georgina sat the children up to milk and a small slice of sultana cake sent over by the kind Shieffield housekeeper, then she bent down and whispered in Timmy's ear. 'You mustn't be rude to Mrs Shieffield, darling. Little boys can't speak to grown up ladies like that. You must always be a little gentleman.'

'I'm sorry, Aunty,' Timmy said quite cheerfully. 'I'll stay out here, shall I? May I have some more cake?'

'Me too,' said Melissa.

Georgina worked swiftly and rejoined Lucinda while the children got down to playing with their toys. Mercifully Timmy was totally non-aggressive with his sister, but rather, sweetly, generously authoritarian.

'I'd go quite crazy looking after those two.' Lucinda sat in a chintz armchair, a small, boneless figure in her exquisite riding gear, which left Georgina wondering where she had left her horse.

'As you say, you're not used to children.'

'And just what is the situation here?' she crooned in that harsh-velvety voice.

'Why, no situation at all.' Georgina didn't even lower her eyes. 'Whatever are you getting at, Mrs Shieffield?'

That same smile stretched over Lucinda's marble skin. 'As I've heard it, your sister-in-law has run off.'

'She certainly has.' Georgina moved back leisurely into her deep armchair, 'to have a holiday.'

'Oh, come, come!'

Georgina stared back with starry, topaz eyes. 'Maybe she was a little upset when she left, but we women are temperamental creatures, aren't we? So much governed by our hormones. I told Jilly to wait a little before she had Melissa, but what can you say to two young people so very much in love? It's a big enough thing adjusting to marriage and a complete change in environment without coping with two demanding little ones as well. I imagine a lot of young wives might fall into a depressive state occasionally. As we've all agreed, Jilly will be all the better for a holiday.'

'You think—*this* will pass over fairly quickly, then?'

'I'm sure of it,' Georgina said boldly. 'I'm here to care for Rick and the children now.'

'And you're not at all what I expected.' Lucinda gave her caricature of a smile. 'Oh, as far as looks go, I'm not surprised. You and your brother are stunningly alike, but you seem a great deal more . . . solid, if you know what I mean.'

'They do say women mature earlier.' Not for anything was Georgina going to lose her calm, contented look. 'You're not eating the cake? It's really delicious.'

'I never eat cake,' Lucinda revealed gently, entering into the game. 'Your brother tells me you're very clever. A journalist, isn't it?'

'I'm with *Profile* magazine,' Georgina told her.

'Really? And what sort of articles do you write to fill up the pages?'

Georgina didn't even fire. 'I'm especially good with people. My last interview was with Professor William Bailey, the economist. You know him?'

'I'm afraid I don't.'

'Oh,' Georgina shrugged lightly, 'he's very highly regarded, both in this country and abroad.'

'Fortunately I don't need anyone to tell me how to control my spending,' said Lucinda. 'So how long do you think your brother ... and your sister-in-law, of course, may have need of you?'

'I can only spare a month.' Georgina sat forward gracefully. 'More coffee?'

'Thank you.'

The coffee was scarcely less black than Lucinda's eyes. 'I doubt if we'll be able to persuade Jilly to stay away that long,' Georgina went on, 'but the point is, she really does need the break. Delayed post-partum problems. Rick had written to me that he was worried that Jilly was feeling low, but a few weeks at Surfers Paradise will put her right.'

'Is that where she is?'

'Near enough,' Georgina smiled. Actually Jilly intended to go north to Noosa, but somewhere along the five-thousand-kilometre coastline was a start. One of the great beauties of Queensland was that it was so huge, twice the size of Texas, which was always thought of as vast. Jilly would be safe.

'You get on well with your sister-in-law, do you?'

'I love her,' said Georgina, realising it was quite true. Her feeling for Jilly went beyond mere affection.

'How unusual!' Lucinda turned her delicate small head, her black gaze far away. 'I don't get on with my sisters-in-law, at all.'

'I didn't even realise Mr Shieffield had sisters, or are you referring to your own family?'

'I'm an only child,' Lucinda said with apparent gratitude. 'My father's heiress. I was speaking about Quinn's two sisters, Anne and Serena.'

'They're married?'

'Yes, thank God, and far away. Anne married Grant Weston, who manages the Territory property for Quinn, and Serena married an American rancher who came out here to see just how we ran things. Quite a romantic encounter. It seems he fell in love with dear Serena on sight.'

'I suppose it does happen,' Georgina agreed.

'Oh, yes, it happens.' Lucinda's strange voice rang like a struck bronze. She turned her face away towards the door, and almost like black magic Quinn Shieffield drove up to confirm it.

The children, who had been playing in the other room, heard the jeep too and they came running, stumbling, into the small parlour. 'It's Mr Shieffield!' Timmy called excitedly while Tiger, shut up in the annexe, began his peculiar howl.

'He's here a little earlier than I expected,' Lucinda said lightly. 'Still, I believe we'll be dining together tonight. So nice of Quinn to ask you.'

'Indeed it was,' Georgina returned warmly. Equality running riot!

Quinn Shieffield was now coming up the stairs and, boss or no, tapped on the frame of the open doorway before Georgina and the children surged out to greet him.

'Hi!' He smiled at Georgina and swung Melissa up. 'Tell me, how is it you get prettier every time I see you?'

Melissa looked at him and gave her special little gurgle.

'Tell me?' He tickled her and she let her head flop over his shoulder.

'I think you're spoiling this child.' Georgina gave him a half-teasing glance. 'I've seen the cuddly little koalas and Timmy's Lego set.'

'All children like presents.' Melissa now had her silky arms twined around his neck.

'What a pretty scene!' Lucinda was standing on the verandah, her tone taunting and scornful.

'Isn't it?' Georgina returned, cool as a cucumber. 'I'll take her now, Mr Shieffield.' She raised her arms, while Melissa, not to be embarrassed, kissed his cheek.

'When are you going to have children of your own, Quinn, anyway?' Lucinda's black eyes narrowed to brilliant slits. But surely that was colour staining her white cheeks.

'I'll take care of it, Lucy, in my own good time.' His tone was so smooth that for a moment Georgina was tricked until she saw his eyes. They were so blue and slashing she almost cried out.

'Well, Tim, what have you been up to?' he asked.

'Showing Aunty around the compound,' Timmy said with an eager smile. 'Will you let her have the jeep one day, Mr Shieffield? Then we can go for a long ride.'

'Now wait a minute, darling!' Georgina protested.

'You can have it right this afternoon.'

'Oh, gee, thanks!'

'Lucky you,' drawled Lucinda. 'I hadn't quite foreseen how like her brother Miss Hamilton is.' She turned to her brother-in-law, gazing at him with an intensity that hovered on despair. 'They've both got that pumpkin-orange hair.'

If she expected Georgina to be mildly affronted Georgina laughed. 'It's never been called that. Amber, tawny, even marmalade, but I guess pumpkin-orange might cover it.'

'It's the most spectacular hair I've ever seen.' Quinn Shieffield gave her a very blue, mocking scrutiny. 'Like the old newly-minted pennies. And even that doesn't describe it.'

'It may turn a very funny shade as you get old,' Lucinda frowned her concern.

'Oh well, I've got a few years before it all catches up with me.' Georgina didn't alter her casual tone in the least. 'If you really mean it, thank you for the jeep, Mr Shieffield.'

'Of course I mean it.' He said it so crisply, she might have been dashed. 'I don't want you to get too far, however. And I want you to use the canopy. The worst of the heat is over, but you're all, officially at least, designated redheads. And while you're here, you can use the pool—teach Melissa to swim. I know Timmy can. In the good times we have superb waterholes. Right now, we're praying for the rain.'

'Rather frightening, isn't it?' said Georgina. 'One hears about drought, but one can't possibly grasp its sheer horror until you see the stock dying and the land reduced to a desert waste. Yet here we seem to be in a comparative oasis.'

'One prepares for the worst times in the best times,' Quinn told her. 'In the best times, it's the Promised Land—in the worst, as close to hell as you'll come. I don't know why I believe it, precisely, but I think the drought will break. And soon. We only need a triggering mechanism as in '67 and '68.'

'Billy says the rain will come too,' Timmy chirruped up.

'Old witch-doctor!' Lucinda muttered, with surprising hostility in her voice.

'Then Billy would know,' Quinn Shieffield passed a hand over Timmy's curly head. 'He's seen this country in its every mood. He knows all its secrets.'

'That's what he says about *you*,' Georgina smiled.

'So he taught me.' For an instant Quinn seemed to respond to the picture Georgina made, all glowing colour and pulsating vitality. He was looking full at her, a certain glint in his burning blue eyes. There was no denying she looked good, her tall, slender figure the ideal clothes-horse. She was only dressed simply, in a voile shirt teamed with just-above-the-knee-length shorts, but she looked amazingly chic as though she was wearing the best of everything. Not even Quinn Shieffield, it seemed, was immune to the long-legged, coltish look as opposed to Lucinda's highly stylised fastidiousness. Georgina looked good in any fabric, but one couldn't imagine Lucinda in anything else but silk, or a light crêpe-de-chine or organza. Hers was not the 'sporty' look, even if she wore her riding clothes well.

Now, behind the mask, she was fiercely restive. 'I really must go,' she said.

'Thank you for coming down to meet me.' Look me over, whatever, Georgina thought.

'I was concerned your that sister-in-law might have walked out and left those two orphans,' Lucinda added.

'What kind of fool remark is that?' Quinn Shieffield said, too quietly, over his shoulder.

'I just had that idea, darling.'

'Mummy's away just for a little while,' Timmy said uncertainly.

Quinn Shieffield nodded. 'And when she's ready to come home,' he promised, 'I'll fly her in.'

The children were delighted to see their aunt go off to a 'party'.

'I wish I be going,' Melissa sighed.

'You'll go to lots of parties, cherub, when you're older.' The two of them were sitting round her as she made up her face.

Melissa, though only a tiny little girl, understood the whole routine, but Timmy sat by in silent amazement.

'Gosh, what a lot of guck,' he said at last, 'but you look lovely. Your eyelashes are so long!'

Georgina turned on the stool and blinked like some mad, mechanical doll, while both the children choked with laughter.

'Now,' she stood up in her pink robe, 'for the dress. I think Mrs Shieffield is rather hoping I'll turn up like a cowcocky, so I'd like to surprise her.'

'What's a cowcocky?' asked Melissa.

'Oh, a country hick. Straw in my hair, darling.'

'It means, Missy,' Tim said kindly. 'it looks like you've been working in a cowshed all day.'

When she was dressed, they all went out into the parlour where Richard was relaxing with a cold beer and some of the new cassettes Georgina had bought him.

At that moment the Little River Band was filling the air.

'Well, what do you think?' Georgina hit his foot down so he would pay attention.

'Oh, mercy!' he simpered, 'ain't those grand folks up at the house gonna be glad to see you!'

'Not too smart?'

'You knock me out,' he chortled, 'And you're my sister! A golden girl. See if you can swing it to marry the boss.'

'Now that's going too far!' Georgina mocked, as much for her benefit as Rick's. In reality she was anything but cool towards Quinn Shieffield. From the very moment she had seen him coming towards her, her blood had started scalding through her veins.

'Well, he's sure making a fuss of you, for heaven's sake,' Rick pointed out blithely.

'I think he's just showing tremendous hospitality to a . . . guest.'

'Even so.' Rick set his daughter on his knee and cuddled her. 'Doesn't Aunty look nice?'

'Lubly!' Melissa agreed gaily.

'I mean, he picked you up. You have the jeep. Now you're having dinner at the house. I could be here one hundred years and I'd never manage that.'

'Well, I'm not an employee, after all,' Georgina pointed out. 'Anyway, part of my job is to interview the man. Gosh, wouldn't he look gorgeous in a picture?'

'So you've noticed,' Rick laughed dryly.

'I've never been blind, brother. He's a very striking man.'

'And dangerous,' Rick warned her suddenly. 'Now you've met Lucinda it can't have escaped you that she considers him hers. Can't you just see her sinking her nails in your beautiful flesh!'

'Careful, Rick!' Georgina's topaz eyes flashed to the children, then back to her brother. 'You've got a little fellow there like a young hawk. Very protective, is our Timmy. Very perceptive too.'

'An' *me!*'

'And you too, darling,' Georgina told her niece tenderly.

At seven o'clock, Quinn Shieffield called for her, amused, admiring, and above all, mocking.

'You have one heck of a beautiful aunt there, Timmy,' he told the smiling little boy.

The most peculiar tension and excitement seemed to go along with them on the short ride. 'It's very kind of you to ask me,' Georgina remarked, trying for her usual composed voice.

'It seemed the friendly thing to do, Miss Hamilton.'

'Please call me Georgina.'

'Perhaps I will,' he glanced briefly at her. 'After dinner.'

A brilliant full moon rode over the house, wrapping the magnificent homestead in a white radiance.

'How fortunate you are,' Georgina said softly, 'to have always lived here. You must love it very much.'

'I'd work myself to death before I'd ever let it go. Responsibilites can be draining, but they're never enough to toss away all a family has stood for. My great-grandfather founded this station with cattle driven overland from New South Wales in a journey that took them four years. He came from a glittering London society to the wilderness of the Wild Heart. Can you imagine what that must have been like? The frightful loneliness, the obstacles? This is a savage land. Its beauty isn't instantly apparently unless one likes primeval beauty and awesome monuments.'

'But the colours!' Georgina exlaimed. 'I always thought the colours Namatjira used in his paintings were too fiery, too vivid to be true, but even from the air it was all there, those fantastic, uncompromising ochres. Incredible reds and yellows and orange, the soft mauves to the hectic purples.'

'You've never seen Ayers Rock?' he asked her.

'No.'

'Then I'll take you. We'll time it for when the Prince and Princess of Wales arrive. With all that Charles has done and seen, this will be a first, and indeed I'm certain they're going to enjoy it—the oldest, geological formation on earth, and for my money the most awesome. Gosse, when he first discovered it little more than a hundred years ago, was staggered by the spectacle ... "the most wonderful natural feature I have ever seen". Seeing it, I assure you, is a lifetime experience—that and the minarets and cupolas of the Olgas, away in the distance. From the air the Rock is like some gigantic prehistoric monster crouching on the endless flat plains of the desert.'

'Then I must see it—while I can,' said Georgina.

'Of course you must.' Quinn stopped the car and glanced at her. 'If you were intending to dazzle me, you've got it just perfect.'

'Well, I didn't, actually,' she said lightly, 'but if I have, so much the better.'

A few moments later they were stepping inside the splendid entrance hall with great chandeliers high up above them spilling light on a photograph that had now come to life. There were the rich furnishings, the deep carpets and the paintings, but the most beautiful and graceful feature was the staircase with its lovely, airy, arched gallery.

'It must give you a great sense of pride to have a home like this,' commented Georgina.

'It's not in my nature to be *too* prideful,' he said mockingly.

'Oh?' She opened her mouth and shut it again. Her first impression of him had been a lordly, sweeping arrogance.

'Frankly, I don't think you believe me.' He was only a little distance away, all bold and smouldering dark good looks. A man to test any woman's mettle.

'As I recall,' she ventured, 'you were ready to label me a simpering fool.'

'My dear Miss Hamilton!' he mocked.

'Don't bother to deny it.' She looked away and upwards, as much to suppress her jumping nerves as to admire the richly adorned ceilings. 'You must think I'm terrible, but is it possible we're dining together? Just the two of us?'

'Well . . .' his expression was amused and mocking again, 'I thought of it.'

'But you weren't sure you could carry the conversation?'

'It all depends what you expect me to say.' He suddenly put out his hand and caught a glowing strand of her hair. 'You must have matched your dress very carefully to your eyes and your hair.'

Georgina had known all along of their sexual attraction, but now its power was vaguely menacing. 'I never undertake to buy a dress without a male friend on hand,' she lied protectively.

'Are you imploring me to believe you?' Quinn pushed the shining strand back into the deep waves that sprang away from her face.

'Oh, there you are, dearest!' a sweet, rather warbling voice exclaimed, and both of them turned, looking up towards the gallery.

'My great-aunt Edwina,' Quinn told Georgina in a voice of the most affectionate indulgence. 'She's been making herself pretty especially for you.'

'So sorry I wasn't here to meet you when you arrived.' The fragile little lady came down the staircase, pleased and excited and wearing her seventy-plus years extraordinarily well. Her long, flowing dress, a flower-printed chiffon, was charmingly old-worlde in style and around her throat she wore a lustrous rope of pearls showing a magnificent diamond and sapphire clasp. 'Such a pleasure dressing up!' She gave Georgina an entirely spontaneous smile. 'We always used to in the old days, but so much has changed! I'm so glad you did, my dear. What *is* that wonderful colour? It's like my bottle of perfume with the light on it.'

'Topaz, deeper?' Quinn Shieffield glanced at Georgina and caught his fragile little great-aunt to him. 'Aunt Edwina, may I present Miss Georgina Hamilton?

Georgina, this is *the* Miss Edwina Shieffield, my grandfather's adored only sister.'

'I never married, you know, dear.' Aunt Edwina looked up into Georgina's face, still smiling entrancingly. 'I was bewildered by so many suitors, Papa thought I should stay with him. So much more comfortable. You're the children's aunt, of course. I couldn't fail to recognise you, with that hair! Wonderful, wonderful! So many people look alike, but one could scarcely miss you. Welcome to Rambulara, my dear.'

'Thank you, Miss Shieffield.' Georgina took the tiny, proffered hand, not just politely, but with a sensation of protectiveness. 'It was very kind of you to invite me. I've never been in such a magnificent house before.'

'Neither have I!' Aunt Edwina exclaimed. 'Papa was a very important man, a man of great character and determination. He *had* to build what he was used to, or at least "a fair chunk of it", as he used to say. I'll tell you, our English cousins live in some style.'

'We're very simple in comparison,' Quinn Shieffield put in lazily.

'With a kingdom of your own?' queried Georgina.

'Oh, I'm going to like you, Miss Hamilton. I feel it.' Aunt Edwina said gaily. 'On second thoughts, I think I'll call you Georgina. It's a lovely name, though I expect you get called Georgie?'

'I do.'

'Well, come in, come in.' The old lady pushed at her flyaway coiffure. 'Why ever were you just standing there in the hall?'

'Admiring the staircase,' Georgina smiled.

'Ah, yes, I know well.' Aunt Edwina turned and looked at her with her blue, far-focused eyes. 'You're seeing yourself as a bride.'

'Bride?' Georgina echoed in astonishment.

'Don't take any notice of Aunt Edwina. She's scary sometimes,' Quinn laughed shortly.

'Sometimes it happens,' Aunt Edwina said vaguely. 'Little premonitions visit me from time to time.'

'So it seems, Georgina,' Quinn told her mockingly, 'you're heading fast towards some whirlwind love affair.'

'I expect it will happen when I'm on one of my trips,' said Georgina.

'It should have to be, I think.'

Aunt Edwina wasn't the only surprise. Georgina was to meet his uncle, Louis Shieffield, and his wife Jennifer, who apparently often stayed there, and a geologist, Ian Forbes, who seemed to be trying to persuade the Shieffields to turn Rambulara into an enormous oil-field. Lucinda Shieffield had sent her apologies—a headache, which didn't sadden Georgina at all.

'You're an intelligent young woman,' Ian Forbes turned to Georgina at one point of the delicious meal. 'What do *you* think?'

'It might be difficult for a cattleman to become an oilman, perhaps?' she ventured.

'The two could exist side by side.'

'Oil doesn't interest me, Ian,' Quinn said mildly.

'It's in pretty short supply.'

'I know. But don't you think being a cattle station is part of Rambulara's charm?'

'You could become the best oil man in the country, I swear.'

'Queensland a second Texas?' An uneasy smile touched Louis Shieffield's firm lips. He was a very distinguished, rather aloof-looking man, a major shareholder in the Shieffield estates but obliged to look to his nephew for the final say. In a way, Georgina decided, it was the same old law of primogeniture. Rambulara, homestead and station, passed to the eldest son. The system, though supposedly abolished, still existed to preserve vast estates. Quinn Shieffield was master of Rambulara, and it would have been the greatest tragedy if he hadn't turned out to be the man he was. At least Louis Shieffield and his more genial wife were unable to say the historic family property wasn't in the best hands. Particularly when their own son, Jonathan, was apparently going through his money in too much of a hurry.

'Would to God he had more of you in him, Quinn,' Louis Shieffield said frankly.

'You were too easy on him, dear,' Aunt Edwina pointed out gently, her blue eyes intent on Louis Shieffield's face. 'I'm not surprised you often feel guilty about it.'

'Really, Aunt!' he protested.

'You, too, Jennifer,' Edwina pointed out astonishingly. 'Forgive me, my dears, but Jonny did need discipline. He never did quite understand that people in our position, more fortunate than others, must develop other things to fall back on than money. Why, Quinn was brought up so strictly. His father never let him fall back on anything.'

'Oh, he did a bit, Edwina,' Quinn smiled slightly and spread his beautifully shaped hands. 'Jon will settle down when he gets married. It's happened before and it will happen again.'

After dinner, when the older people were comfortably settled in the more intimate dimensions of the library, Georgina had a short interval with her host.

'Would you like to look around the rest of the house?' he invited.

'I'd love to.'

Aunt Edwina nodded her gauzy silver head. 'Don't get a fright if you run into Lucinda.'

With the greatest difficulty Georgina stifled a laugh. Aunt Edwina Shieffield spoke with the freedom and frankness of a child.

'Naughty, Edwina,' Quinn told her without a hint of reproach. He took Georgina's elbow and ushered her out of the soft opulence of the room with its walls of bookshelves ceiling-high. 'You must never be surprised by what my Aunt Edwina says,' he warned gently. 'In many ways she's lived in a closed world. She was handicapped by a serious illness in her childhood that left her a little slower than the rest of us, but her intelligence should never be underestimated. In many ways, she's as sharp as a tack.'

'I'm sure she is,' Georgina said warmly. 'She seemed to grasp most of what was said tonight.'

'Not one of us can accept the idea of turning Rambulara into a series of oil rigs, though we're fairly certain it's there in vast quantities. But it's never been a viable proposition up until now.'

'Either way you're sitting on a fortune,' Georgina mused.

'I prefer cattle and a natural landscape,' he observed detachedly. 'Now, shall we start on our tour of exploration?'

'By all means. It must have been a wonderful place to hide as a child.'

'My sisters could tell you,' he smiled. 'I never had time to forget I was the son and heir. The girls used to bring their friends home from boarding school, six or seven at a time. They all wanted to come, so they were brought out in relays. The worst years were when they were drowning in girlish dreams.'

'You mean when they were telling each other you were awfully rich and handsome?'

'How do you mean, *were*?'

She could feel his tall presence beside her as a kind of violent magnetism that drew tingles from her whole body. The lady novelists spoke of electricity that crackled along the nerve centres, but it was proving to be agonisingly accurate. She had never been so conscious of another human being in her life. 'What a lovely room you have here,' she said a little shakily as he threw open a door.

'The Garden Room, we always call it, though the gardens aren't too impressive at the moment. Bore water is no substitute for rain. My grandmother tried for years to grow the kind of plants she had lived with all her life, but Gloucestershire isn't the Australian Outback. In the end she had to go native, or at least exotic. Either way, as she was a great gardener, the results were spectacular. She listed hundreds of native plants I don't think anyone ever bothered with before, then found they were superb in Gran's massed displays. Billy, as it happens, told her where to find water and the two of them used to walk all over deciding where they were going to sink shafts. They were an odd couple—my grandmother, tall and sprightly, in one of the enormous coolie hats she always wore, and Billy always trailing her about four paces behind. When she died he went walkabout for weeks. Don't ask me how, but he knew to the minute when she would die. He's been with my family nearly all his life, but it was Gran who had his absolute devotion. She was the first one to see the cave hunting scenes—a great honour. Not even my grandfather knew they existed. In fact he wasn't all that happy that he hadn't been allowed to see them first. Strange in a way, because in the aboriginal culture its the man who counts. Women are excluded from all their important ceremonies.'

'Obviously the aboriginals haven't got it on their own. Not too many men don't believe in the divine right of the male. Black or white and all shades in between.' Georgina turned so that the light slid along the soft, fluid lines of her amber-coloured dress. It was simple in style, everything was in the cut, and no one without a young, beautiful body could have worn it.

'And not a smart man among them who'd underestimate a woman's power,' Quinn returned a little tautly, his blue eyes tracking the path of the light along her body. 'Don't you think, on the evidence, we *are* superior?'

'Could it have something to do with female suppression?' she retorted, not controlling her quick temper too well. 'I don't equate superiority with higher status. Males do have that and exercise it to the hilt.'

'Do you fear men?' he asked gently.

'Don't be ridiculous!'

'I think you do, a little. Not so much that they might

threaten what you want to do, but that they might want to make too much of you.'

'Could you explain that?' She had wandered away from him, as one moves when confronted with someone one can't handle.

'You're terrified of your own attraction,' he told her.

'Good grief!' she laughed innocently, aware he had discovered something about her she was always in flight from.

'Come back here then.'

'Why?' Here too the walls were covered with the most beautiful pictures, Impressionists, modern, but her vision seemed to be frozen.

'Oh,' Quinn laughed briefly, 'to amaze me. It's not such a great thing, after all, to be a beautiful woman. To so delight the eye you learn very early to be defensive.'

It was so true she turned to look at him as though he had spoken aloud forbidden words. 'You make me sound quite without poise!' she protested.

'Not at all. You're very bright and determined, but at the sexual level you run away.'

'I see,' she said tautly. 'What do you have in mind?'

'My dear Miss Hamilton!' he mocked her. 'Absolutely no advances.'

'Thank God for that!' She picked up a small bronze and set it down again. 'I thought you were working up to something.'

'It wouldn't suit you?' He came and stood just behind her.

'Emphatically the answer is, *no!*'

'Liar,' he laughed. 'After all, I'm as attracted to you as you are to me.'

'So what happens next?' she swung about and asked him in a half-lively, half-angry voice.

'We'll have a look at the other room,' he said gently. 'It's right through that door.'

He was playing some game, of course he was. But Georgina wasn't about to let him break a single rule.

He was used to having anything he wanted. She knew quite well that that included women, and that was what frightened her.

They toured most of the house, endlessly tilting at one another, an exercise so confusing, so exciting, she thought her blood must be on fire and her eyes glowing wildly. Quinn was everything she had ever wanted in a man. But too much besides. Her best course would be to beat a hasty withdrawal, then go to sleep and dream about him.

'I expect we should be getting back to the others,' she said firmly.

'You think they might be wondering what we're up to?'

'I can't tell you. I don't know you all that well.'

'Would you come riding with me tomorrow? You do ride, your brother told me.'

'I'd like to,' her creamy skin was flushed, 'but I can't possibly leave the children.'

'Lulah will look after them for an hour or two,' he said dryly. 'In fact they're very fond of her, and she of them. She went halfway down to meet you this afternoon then scampered back with shyness.'

'Why,' Georgina turned back and smiled, 'please tell her to come. No one could be nervous of *me*!'

'Oh?' He put out his hand and tilted her chin up. 'My blood pressure's been charging up for the last hour.'

'Forget it,' she warned, fighting the dazzlement of those iridescent eyes.

'I don't think I know what you mean, Miss Hamilton.'

'*You* know,' she whispered, her heart fluttering madly. 'I suppose you're bored enough to start a bit of drama.'

So engrossed were they, they didn't notice Lucinda until she finally almost snarled, 'One more conquest to notch up, darling?' She stepped gracefully into the room in a sort of beautiful-wicked-witch's outfit that was unbelievably spectacular for bed. It was silvery-grey and with the light through it excitingly insubstantial.

'Why, Lucinda,' Quinn greeted her suavely, so suavely it was the best recovery Georgina had ever seen, 'you almost gave us heart failure! What on earth are you doing, wandering about with your bad head?'

'I heard voices.' She came to stand beside him, looking up at him. She was very small, very feline, her body curved.

'You did? From inside a four-inch-thick cedar door?'

Lucinda's bitter little smile flickered a moment. 'Don't be angry with me, darling, for interrupting your little scene!'

'Perhaps you can tell us what a *scene* means?' Georgina said smartly with her usual impulse to plunge in. This woman was dangerous, a fool could see that, but she wasn't going to permit herself to be intimidated.

'Must you explode like that, Miss Hamilton?' Lucinda purred. 'I don't blame you at all for being disappointed. You want what everyone else wants, but before you take off your clothes...'

'God, Lucy, you disgust me,' Quinn Shieffield dropped his hand to his sister-in-law's shoulder and spun her around.

'You'll break my bones, Quinn!' Lucinda cried, yet she was tipping her body towards him as though begging him to pull her into his arms. 'Oh, you're beautiful, Miss Hamilton,' she hurled at Georgina, 'but that's not enough. I *know!*'

'Shut up, Lucy,' Quinn muttered, and *did* pull her to him. 'Would you mind finding your own way downstairs, Georgina?' he said harshly. 'My sister-in-law is just barely sober.'

'You swine, Quinn!' Lucinda was nuzzling her head into his chest.

Looking at them, Georgina stepped hurriedly away. She had never in her life been aware of such passion, and now it was touching her. 'I'm sorry,' she said quietly. 'Of course I can find my own way back.'

'Yes, go away.' Lucinda lifted her raven head and blew Georgina a kiss. 'You have to go, really. They all do.'

CHAPTER SIX

BY morning Georgina had well and truly decided she was no match for Quinn Shieffield or his astounding sister-in-law. For twenty-four years of her life she had kept out of the fast lane, now she was too timid to try it. So she had reacted to Quinn on sight? He was a very special person. And obviously she wasn't the only female guest who immediately flipped as soon as he looked at her. The great thing was to accept that such people existed, like characters on the television, but it could never be her world. Her world was many things, but most of all she craved serenity. Just coming to Rambulara had complicated her life enormously.

Lulah presented herself at the bungalow, mid-morning, a dusky, sixteen-year-old charmer with huge, liquid black eyes and the merry smile that was so characteristic of her people.

'So this is Lulah,' said Georgina, and Lulah, as soon as she saw the quality of Georgina's smile, slipped inside the door.

'Mornin', Miss Georgie.'

'Show Aunty how you stand like a bird,' Timmy said.

Lulah did her imitation of a brolga so perfectly they all broke into laughter. It was somehow very touching to see Melissa embrace her, and Georgina realised that Lulah, too, was very much affected by the little children's friendship.

The morning went smoothly. Lulah kept the children happily occupied with lots of paper and crayons; Lulah was, in fact, a talented artist, and Georgina turned her attention to finishing a few of the jobs Jilly had started. There was a freight plane coming in this afternoon, so it could take her long letter to Jilly out. She had managed to finish it off when she arrived back at the bungalow last night. Jilly might have nearly worked herself into a nervous breakdown over Rick's infatuation with Lucinda Shieffield, but that would pass as quickly as it had come. Jilly had never seen Lucinda when her control had snapped. Georgina had, and it still made her shiver every time she thought about it. Lucinda, dangerous and trembling in Quinn's arms. There seemed something terribly sick about her passion, like a poison. And what of Quinn Shieffield? Wasn't there some grim delight in the way he had jerked her into his arms? They did carry that primitive aura, an indicator of the kind of passions most people were afraid of, not just Georgina. Letting a man like Quinn Shieffield into her life was like watching an eagle swoop on a dove.

By two o'clock, she was certain even Quinn Shieffield had thought better of taking her riding. When she went, and she was looking forward to it enormously, she would go with Rick. It was a lovely, secure feeling knowing Lulah was so good with the children, and she carried a little air of authority from her years in charge of the younger children at her church mission. Georgina was certain Lulah would prove utterly reliable, as indeed she turned out to be.

As soon as Georgina decided she could begin to relax the jeep pulled up in front of the bungalow. It was Quinn Shieffield and he came straight up the steps, his smile a little taut, his attraction destructive.

'Well, aren't you ready?'

'What for?' Georgina asked abruptly.

'This afternoon we're going riding, Miss Hamilton.'

She shook her splendid mane. 'I thought you'd decided to resist the urge.'

'Where are the children?' He turned his head.

'Melissa has a long nap in the afternoons,' Georgina explained. 'Timmy, too, seems to have fallen over. Not for long, though, I expect.'

'And Lulah?' he frowned.

'Lulah's magic with the children,' said Georgina.

'She's making a cup of tea for us at the moment. Did you want to speak to her?'

'I will.' He gave her a paradise-blue glance. 'While you change that skirt for a pair of jeans or whatever.'

'We're going, then?' Despite herself she bit her lip.

'My dear girl,' he said tightly, 'if you think you're irresistible, you're not.'

'Great!' Instead of being offended, she smiled. 'Just how many susceptible women do you get out here anyway?'

'A lot.' He could have at least worn a shirt that wasn't a beautiful blue colour.

'Well, either you have it or you haven't,' she mocked over her shoulder. 'Would you like to wait in the parlour? I'll send Lulah to you.'

They rode out into the rugged, rose-pink sandhill country, where the spinifex stood in great spherical clumps. Except for a few scattered trees, acacias and white-barked eucalyptus, the shifting hills were bare. Quinn swerved his horse, a magnificent creature of polished ebony, to avoid a great lizard that suddenly darted from one clump of spinifex to the other, while Georgina leaned back in the saddle staring up at the incredible legions of swirling birds. She would have believed such a sight to be rare, yet it was commonplace for the Outback. The budgerigars flew in tight formation, waves of green and gold with touches of azure blue near the beak; hundreds of tiny crimson chats and some other variegated little bird, considerably more colourful. There were splendid parrots as well, and two feet away from them a pink and pearl grey galah came to roost on a tree. Now it turned about to peer at her, inquisitive, not the least afraid.

'How terrible that people capture them to sell overseas,' Georgina murmured.

'They don't do any capturing around here,' Quinn told her. 'Some people will do anything for money. Our beautiful birds fetch a huge price overseas, but it's illegal, as you know. The Golden Shoulder of the Far North is one of the rarest and most beautiful birds in the world, yet they get drugged and stuffed in cans and smuggled out of the country to some rich collector. With a country so big and so empty it's difficult to police.'

'And, I hear, dangerous.'

'There are always dangerous men in remote places.'

Georgina looked quickly over her shoulder and saw he was wearing his mocking smile.

'Relax, Georgina. Imagine you're back home, riding with a friend.'

'You don't seem to fit that description,' she commented.

'Friend?' His blue eyes beneath the wide brim of his hat, flashed bright.

'You didn't happen to think any more about my interviewing you?'

'Take it easy, Georgina,' he said dryly, 'One thing at a time.'

'I haven't got all that much time,' she reminded him. 'My boss will expect me to send back some powerful stuff.'

'Surely to God there's a hero around here some place. Bruce Winton from Windarra is a great guy.'

'Ah, yes—I've met him.'

'I know.'

'You didn't mention it,' she said.

'This isn't the place for secrets, Miss Hamilton. Everyone knows everyone else's business. They hear it discussed over the two-way radio.'

'Then everyone must know I'm here—and why.'

'Surely you're here for business and pleasure?' he queried.

'I guess so.' Georgina stared ahead of her at the heat haze. It hung like a shimmering silver-blue curtain that lifted as one rode towards it. It was an indescribable sensation, quite unique in all her life, to be moving through this ancient, uncompromising landscape, the walkabout route of the aborigines since the Dreamtime.

Accustomed to the lush tropical vegetation of the State capital as she was, this part of Rambulara was as arid and desolate as the far side of the moon. But for the colours! The brilliant, enamelled colours of the birds' plumage, the magnificent baked-in colours of the incredibly ancient land. It was all so immense, so silent, Georgina had the strange sensation that her own world was no more and she had gone back in time to the Creation when the world was molten and the great monuments were being fashioned.

'Right now I'd like to have a camera!' Quinn rode up to her and said.

'Me too.' She turned back to him laughingly. 'This is a photographer's dream. It's so savage and so splendid!'

'Actually I was considering more your face. It looks as though it's been touched by some magic.'

'That,' Georgina nodded, 'and power. I never imagined there was such space or such a quality of silence—I'm conscious of the slightest noise. The wind sliding past my face, the call of a bird. There can't be any chance one would want to live in a city after this.'

His expression seemed to harden. 'Some people are frightened half to death. Oh yes, it's fantastic, astonishing, incredible. But alien, always alien.'

'It's certainly different,' Georgina agreed, 'but I would never be afraid.'

'You should be. The Inland is full of threats. Even today one could die only half an hour by car from Alice Springs itself. The sun generates temperatures of forty-three degrees and more and the atmosphere is so dry any man or woman who found themselves stranded through breakdown either in a car or plane would have maybe a day to live. The desert *is* magic, *I* think so, but irredeemably cruel. Only the aborigines and a few hardy animals know how to survive.'

'I'm going to get an article out of Billy,' she said.

'*What?*' His deeply blue eyes were amused.

'He's a wonderful old man, and what he doesn't know about this country doesn't matter.'

'Agreed, Miss Hamilton,' he drawled serenely. 'I was thinking more you mightn't get him to talk.'

'Oh, he'll talk to *me*,' Georgina said seriously. 'He knows I'm so interested.'

'Well then, so you are!' He smiled a little crookedly. 'Come on, Georgina, I want to show you the cave.'

By the time they reached the rock shelter Georgina felt hot and breathless and not a little rattled, the causes of which she preferred not to dwell on. It had not been an impossible climb, neither had it been particularly easy. She would probably have relished it as a tomboyish teenager or then again with Rick, but it was infinitely less disturbing to claw for handholds and scramble for footholds than to have Quinn Shieffield seize one and pin one to his rock-hard chest. He fairly made her feel faint and her legs go rubbery. It even reminded her of an old Valentino movie where the increasingly susceptible heroine was being swept up by a force clearly stronger than anything she had ever known in her life. There was even a resemblance in the hero's blazing eyes; though Valentino's had been a smouldering black and Quinn Shieffield's were as blue as sapphires.

'You're out of condition, Miss Hamilton.' He looked down at her, arrogant black head thrown back.

'The devil I am!' she puffed. 'It's all these little pebbles.'

'Sure it's not too far up?' He held out his hand.

'Oh, why are you such a pure, unadulterated bully?'

'Never. Not with girls.' He steadied her while she stood weakly. 'Look out, Georgina.' He indicated the great vista.

'I know. It's wonderful.' She turned her head. 'The Timeless Land.'

'You almost sound like my kind of woman,' he said with a look of mockery.

'Oh?' She lifted a dark, delicate eyebrow. 'I'd like to talk to you about . . . women. You must be one of the most eligible bachelors in the country.'

'It would be foolish to deny it,' he shrugged.

'I won't take up a great deal of your time,' she pointed out earnestly. 'You know it could be a very good story.'

'No story, Miss Hamilton,' he said.

'Please?' She lifted her topaz eyes, enjoying a moment of dangerous flirtation.

'Did you come to talk or see the cave?'

'The cave,' she said brightly. 'Right away.'

Even then she was totally unprepared for the strange radiance and power that streamed from the ancient rock paintings. She backed away from the cave walls, making soft little exclamations all the time. Her head seemed to be buzzing and her blood tingled. She had never been so conscious of the great antiquity of her own country, nor come into direct contact with the visual art of its aboriginal people. Now she was privileged to view an outstanding gallery, and she moved around the gloomy cave, quiet as though hypnotised.

'Here, have the torch,' Quinn said behind her.

'How old would these paintings be?' she asked. The golden circle of light tracked human beings, animals, trees, birds, many abstract symbols impossible to interpret but extraordinarily effective in the design.

'Their antiquity is under discussion at the moment. So far as Professor Matthew Green is concerned they belong to a prehistoric culture period. They're obviously very, very old, and according to the oldest aboriginal surviving in my grandfather's time, the fact of their existence had been handed down from antiquity. This is a sacred site and the drawings are an excellent example of aboriginal art.'

'But surely that's a crocodile?' Georgina pointed to, but did not touch a powerful drawing of a long, reptilian creature. 'A crocodile around here?'

'There *were* crocodiles in the Centre up until Pleistocene times. It was no myth about the inland sea. There are all kinds of fossilised sea creatures embedded in the desert rocks. It certainly does look like a crocodile, or it could be a highly stylised X-ray drawing. All the experts who've been here are in agreement about one thing: the paintings are all very, very old and they're quite remarkable. They certainly bring this cave to life. Shine the torch up on the roof. The figures aren't as fantastic as the famous Wondjina paintings from the Kimberleys . . .'

'You mean the space men Von Danniken said they represented?'

'If you saw them, you'd know why he said it. They look for all the world like astronauts in their gear, especially the big oval band that encircles the face . . .'

'Oh, I love that female figure with the headdress!' Georgina exclaimed, tipping her head right back the better to see it. 'And there's the companion male.'

'Mythical beings, male and female, guardians of the local aborigines,' said Quinn.

'And all those other little creatures?' Georgina touched the light to the surrounding beings.

'The totemic beings associated with the guardian creatures. There are other sites on Rambulara, but mostly the drawings have to do with sorcery and love magic. These are the great Spirit beings above the concerns of mere mortals.'

'They're beautiful,' said Georgina, and he nodded.

'Consider yourself honoured.'

'I do.'

'There's something about you, Georgina, that puts me in a good mood,' he told her.

'Thank you.' She heard the amusement and mockery in his voice; but more, the ring of truth. 'I could stay here for ages.'

'No, we have to go. There *is* trying to get you down again. I remember climbing Ayers Rock once with a seventy-eight-year-old woman and she seemed to float up that difficult climb, but I thought we'd have to get a helicopter to get her off.'

'Well, what happened? Did she fall down?'

'Not exactly, but *I* was ready to by the time we reached the bottom! It's one hell of a climb for anyone, let alone an old lady, but she told me later it was like having a marvellous adventure.'

'Are you going to let *me* climb it?' Georgina asked.

'Not on what I've seen.'

They stepped outside the cave and the brilliance of the sun made them blink. The branches of a feathery little acacia arched across the entrance, and as Georgina looked back she reflected that the narrow entrance was so well hidden, so isolated, one could live a lifetime on the station and never realise it was there. She could see the horses standing almost motionless on the level ground, and the blue glare was so strong there were lakes of crystal clear water shining through the stunted trees.

'Give me your hand.' Quinn stepped down the slope and looked up at her.

'And have us both career down? No way!' The difficulty wasn't the height but the extraordinary nature of the terrain, so ancient and weathered, blood-red rocks broke up under one's tread, and gravel flowed like lava to the ground, half prompting Georgina to shriek with terror. She would go anywhere where she could get a secure footing, but this was every bit as precarious as treading an ice valley. She had never been so concerned about where she placed her feet. On the other hand, Quinn was moving as he always did, with latent power and confidence. Of course, he had been treading these eroded slopes since he had been a boy.

'Ah!' she wailed suddenly.

'It's all right, I've got you!' he reassured her, a shade impatiently.

'You don't have any other wonderful tricks, do you, like walking across burning stones?'

'You're being too careful, don't you see? You're losing confidence. If it wasn't so damned steep I'd carry you.'

'I expect that's what you said to the old lady?'

'Fortunately she was half your size,' he drawled.

'Damn it all, I never go much over eight stone,' Georgina said snappily, quite missing the glance he rested on her.

'When the rains come,' he said vibrantly, 'all those miles of sand-gravel flats will be covered with wildflowers.'

'How wonderful!' She stopped breathlessly and had to catch his side. 'Isn't there some poem about the white and golden glory of the daisy-patterned plains?'

'If there isn't there ought to be. The wildflowers in the Channel Country are glorious—white, gold, pink, purple, scarlet. You haven't seen anything until you see the desert bloom. When I was two or three or four, my father used to take me up before him and ride out to where the desert came alive. Miles and miles of the pink parakeelya with its thick, fleshy leaves, paper daisies extending right to the horizon.'

'You have your memories,' she said gently, moved by something she saw in his face.

'They last for ever.' Quinn lowered his head and looked down at her, the bronze of his skin enhancing the intense blue of his eyes. They were flame, not flower, and she wasn't accustomed to the depth of his regard. As a good-looking girl she was used to the bright appreciation she saw reflected in male eyes, but Quinn Shieffield seemed to look beyond the superficial right through to what some people called the spirit and others the soul. She could feel herself responding to him, her body melting, like the sun on ice.

'When we get to the bottom, we'll celebrate,' he told her.

'Oh, *how?*'

'You don't really need to be told, do you?' He pivoted with his quick, panther-like grace.

Excitement and confusion stirred Georgina to a strange recklessness. She had been desperately drawn to Quinn from the moment she had seen him forging towards her at the air terminal. It was if all her life had

only been a prelude to their meeting, yet obviously he
could hurt her. There could be no real relationship.
Probably he was a hunter by instinct, and something
about her had aroused his desire.

He reached out his hand to help her, but she pulled
back. 'I'm all right.'

And she would have been. Yet as she reached down
to secure a handhold she disturbed the resting place of a
large sandhill lizard who stood up on its legs and hissed
at her.

'Oh—help us!' She threw herself backwards, almost
violently, and the angry lizard instead of scuttling away
seemed bent on biting her. Did lizards bite?

'Georgina, what the hell!' exclaimed Quinn.

'Get back,' she yelled, 'it's a lizard!'

A hurtling stone struck her painfully in the back, but
still the lizard came on, rising slightly on its webbed feet
as though it was going to unravel a long forked tongue
at her.

'Go away!' she said in a strangled whisper, and made
a throwing-away motion at the miniature monster, but
it closed on her as though, like the giant goanna, it was
going to run up her body. The idea was too horrible to
be borne. She stood up frantically, lifting her hands
sharply, and as she did so, the earth seemed to move
from under her and she went thrashing wildly down the
slope.

'Georgina!'

She heard Quinn's fierce cry, then because he flung
himself in her path they were rolling together, his arms
locked tightly around her body, so she was really not
suffering any harm at all.

At last they lost momentum and stopped.

'My God!' he muttered turbulently. 'Are you all
right?'

'I think so,' Georgina murmured, breathing carefully. 'You ought to be gratified we got down so
quickly.'

'I thought you were supposed to be intelligent?' He

looked down at her slender body, free now of his crushing grasp.

'I think I left it back home,' she said shakily. 'Great hissing lizards aren't everyone's cup of tea.'

'When the poor things are harmless?' He was removing bits of debris from her hair.

'Are they really harmless? I thought it was trying to bite me.'

'Clearly all your shrieking had it rattled.' He picked up her arm and examined the scraped elbow. 'I should say you were lucky.'

'I was. *You* were there.' Her voice was low, but penetratingly sweet. 'I'm sorry, I know I was rather stupid.'

'Incredibly stupid, if you must know,' he agreed.

'And I've paid for it.' She sat up looking briefly at her grazes. 'I suppose you'll think it a good idea not to bring me again.'

'I might,' his blue eyes slid over her, 'if you weren't so damned amusing. Get back!' he mimicked her, 'it's a *lizard!* I understand you were trying to protect me.'

'Of course I was,' she said with an air of bravery. 'Oh, I think I've hurt my back.'

'Where?' Instantly his mocking smile was gone. He held her shoulder and gently turned her. 'There's blood on your blouse.'

'Oh, heavens!' she said anxiously. 'Much?'

'Here, show me.' Without so much as asking her permission he separated her shirt from her jeans.

'Oh, please, *no!*' she protested modestly.

'Shut up!'

'I was only trying to be modest.'

'I *know* you are,' he said abruptly. He pushed her shirt up and inspected the slight wound. 'You're going to need some antiseptic on that.'

'Is it bad?' she queried, peering round.

'Actually, *no.*' Quinn lowered her shirt and his hand seemed to slip around her waist, resting against her bare skin. 'You understand, don't you, that I want a reward?'

'Anything. Nothing's too much.' She smiled so he would know it was all banter, yet his hand against her skin was enormously disturbing.

'All right. I want to make love to you.'

She shook her head. 'I'm sorry—too dangerous.' Her voice was just barely controlled.

'You don't trust me?'

'Nor *me*.'

Quinn leaned down very suddenly and took her full bottom lip gently between his teeth.

'No,' she breathed into his mouth.

He put his arm around her and tipped her whole body right into his arms. '*Yes*.' He was just barely tasting her lips, inhaling the fragrance of her hair and her skin. 'You're in a tough spot, Miss Hamilton.'

'And you're no gentleman, Mr Shieffield!'

'You know why? Because you encourage me too much.'

'I don't!'

He let her deny it, his mouth covering the soft skin of her cheek, under-chin and throat. It was so beautiful, it was anguish.

'I'm insane,' she said raggedly, 'and this is a terrible way for you to act.'

'I thought I was being rather gallant?'

Some little element of mockery made her quick temper flare. 'I told you, Mr Shieffield, I didn't come here for you to seduce me.'

'Well, that's what *I've* been since I sighted a pair of topaz eyes and all that beautiful hair!' Quinn grasped a curling handful and tilted her head right back into the curve of his shoulder. 'I'm going to kiss you, Georgina. No big deal.'

It was the biggest deal of her life. Her heart rose into her throat, then seemed to stop. Why was she allowing him to enfold her in his arms? Why was she allowing him to cover her mouth, to open it? Her head seemed to be filled with brilliant light. She was weak with mingled shock and desire; utterly a soft creature, helpless against his driving strength.

Her hand was moving against his chest with a gesture of resistance, but the slow melting feeling was turning abruptly to wildfire, so voluptuous it was unbearable to her. If only she could keep some semblance of control— but the whole world was swinging out of focus . . . it was no longer there. She was into some strange, new country one sometimes visited in dreams; a place full of fear and wonder.

Quinn was exploring her mouth deeply, with a dizzying desire and curiosity, forcing her to meet his passion with her own. Her blood was flaming through her veins, and this drove her to hit out at him, a succession of small-fisted thuds against his chest, that for long, long, heart-stopping moments he ignored, his mouth, arms, strong and demanding, his desire to possess her sweeping him on.

'Quinn, please!' She dragged her mouth away, the peaks of her breasts taut against the thin fabric of her shirt. If he touched her there, if he slipped his hand under her shirt and ran it up over her breast, she could find herself destroyed.

'Dear God!' he groaned briefly, and lifted his head. 'Give up. Give in.'

Her small face was very white, exaggerated by the luxuriant glowing nimbus of her hair. All trace of lip colour was gone from her softly bruised mouth and her topaz eyes were so brilliant they looked fevered. She looked startlingly beautiful and infinitely sexual.

'Do I take it you have an objection?' Quinn asked casually, but even then the mockery was a caricature of itself. He too looked different, the bold, striking face carved into severity.

'Yes.' She said it faintly, very faintly.

'Because you're virtuous or only frightened?'

'Both.'

A pulse was beating crazily in her throat and he pressed a finger to it, his hand a deep bronze against her flawless white skin. Her luminous eyes seemed to be regarding him with a certain awe and puzzlement, and she was so white he was concerned for her.

'You're not going to faint on me, are you, Georgina?'

She shook her head but didn't speak.

'I didn't think anything could move you to total silence,' he tried for lightness. 'At least smile to reassure me.'

Her golden glance wavered and the tip of her pink tongue came out to moisten her full mouth. 'Don't pay any attention to me,' she whispered huskily. 'I feel a bit odd—I expect it's the fall.'

'It can't be the fact I kissed you?'

'Don't be stupid!' she blinked. 'I've been kissed frequently since I was sixteen.'

'I'll rephrase my question. But you've never been so ... shaken?' Carefully he moved her into a more comfortable position.

'Well, you didn't exactly kiss me like everybody else. In fact,' and now the colour washed over her delicate, high cheekbones, 'you kiss like a heathen!'

'Lovely!' He laughed, bent his head and brushed her mouth lightly. 'So do you. You have a golden, wholesome brightness about you, yet you weave a powerful, all-encompassing spell. You'll have to be careful how you use it.'

'Oh, I will. You wait and see!'

'Really?' His startlingly blue eyes lit up.

'What conceited creatures you men are!' Georgina declared, trying to sit up and needing assistance. 'If you think I'm a push-over, my dear Mr Shieffield, you've got another think coming!'

'Of course! All the desire was on my side.'

'Most of it,' she amended.

'Would you like me to catch you out on that lie?' He put his two hands on her shoulders, tipped her back coolly and kissed her an inch from her beautiful, slanting eyes.

'You stop that!' she said shakily, before she yielded. 'You may not like it, but you *were* losing a bit of your iron control.'

'A bit? The lot!' he admitted briskly. 'Get up, little girl, while you can.' He bent over her and lifted her to her feet. 'It's humiliating, isn't it, the risk of abandonment?'

'I don't want to abandon myself.' Georgina told him sternly, 'except to my future husband.'

'Oh, splendid, Miss Hamilton!' he applauded her. 'Sentiments I can only admire. If you want to consider me for husband material, go ahead.'

His expression said it all. 'I'm sorry,' Georgina said tartly, 'I'd never dream of looking so high.' She went to stalk past him and he pulled her back against him.

'You're the only woman to reject me, if nothing else.'

It was shattering to be so close to his lean, hard body. 'That's not what *I've* heard,' she retaliated unwisely.

'No?' Quinn glanced down at her. 'Tell me about it.'

'Not today.' She had instantly regretted her lapse.

'Don't care to repeat the gossip?' He looked contemptuous and high-mettled.

'I daresay it wasn't true.'

'Was it delivered with malice?' He held her by the shoulder while she answered.

'Not at all. Just filling in the gaps, nothing else.' What had it do to with her that Quinn Shieffield had once been engaged to his own sister-in-law; that the same sister-in-law now lived under his roof and looked at him with a peculiar, sick avidity.

'Are you afraid to tangle with me, Miss Hamilton, after all?'

'You know I am.' She didn't say it nervously, or provocatively, but with a grave sincerity, and he answered it with a terrible, ironic bow.

CHAPTER SEVEN

AFTER that, Georgina saw little of Quinn, and it seemed to matter so terribly that instead of her moping it had the effect of bringing her to almost frantic life. With Lulah and the children she arranged trips every day. They all strode around, even Melissa tried to keep up, as if they had to cram the adventures and experiences of a lifetime into a handful of weeks. Lulah, and Billy, when he could be persuaded to join them, were fascinating companions, connecting every landmark, every secret trail, every animal, with some tribal legend. They encountered no problems, because after all, they didn't venture that far, but all their journeys sealed Georgina and the children deeper and deeper into love for this vast, sacred land.

Often they picknicked beneath the river gums and while the children dropped off to sleep for short intervals Billy or Lulah began to open their hearts to this little girl who was really very understanding and seriously, deeply interested in their culture and concept of life. In a way it was a thank-you gesture to Georgina for treating them with a respect not all local people accorded them, and they knew, too, that perhaps Georgina would speak for their people if they gave her the answers to all her various questions. Above all the aboriginal did not need what other peoples needed for a satisfying life. The material possessions, the amassing of a great number of them, had little to do with making an aboriginal happy. Nor for that matter did it make the people of Western European culture completely happy. Far more crucial to their happiness was land; their basic need to be as one with nature. It was only contact with the white man that had upset a system, basically conservative, that had worked admirably from

95

antiquity until white settlement began. For a people so remote and secluded from all others the white conquest of the Continent had come as a tremendous cultural shock. Since then, as always, the weak had to bow to the strong. The impact of the outside world on the aborigines had been devastating. Their world broke up before them, and with the growth of settlement, they were forced into pockets in the remote areas, forced into a way of life that could not have differed more from their own, and so the myth of their inferiority began. Some were more fortunate than others; those who could turn to the land owners for support in the social and economic sense. Aboriginal stockmen formed the backbone of the far-flung, giant cattle stations, and from all Georgina had learned, the Shieffield family, right from the time of the Hon. George Arthur, had concerned themselves with the health, education and general well-being of the aboriginal people on their vast property as well as providing employment. In a sense the family had served as a buffer between the native people and the less friendly outside world. On Rambulara, at least, they had the illusion of leading the traditional life. Also, more importantly, they retained their self-esteem. Georgina, in her long talks with Lulah and Billy, concerned herself primarily with finding out just how happy, or unhappy, they were with their modified way of life. Given, they were better off than most. They were housed, fed and clothed and drew wages; they were close to their natural environment, their spiritual life was respected, but they were not terribly receptive at the material level. So far as Georgina was concerned both Lulah and Billy were very quick and alert and possessed extra senses she found quite uncanny. For instance, both of them became aware of Lucinda's impending presence when she was virtually invisible to the naked eye. At these times, they simply melted away; a wise move, considering the kind of treatment Lucinda meted out to them.

That particular morning as Georgina was recording a long, satisfying conversation with Lulah on what avenues she considered open to her as a young, educated, aboriginal girl, her ambitions generally, including her thoughts of marriage and motherhood, her possible acceptance in a wider community, Lulah suddenly jumped up, leaned across the table and said to the startled Georgina: 'I'm off, Miss Georgie!'

'That's all right, Lulah,' Georgina smiled reassuringly, 'I expect I'm tiring you with all my questions.'

'It's not you, miss,' Lulah touched the back of Georgina's hand. 'I know I shouldn't say this, but that Miss Lucinda spooks me out.'

'Lucinda!' Georgina stood up and stared around hard. It was slightly unsettling the way Lulah and Billy homed in on Lucinda's magnetic field. 'You mean she's around some place?'

'She's thinkin' about you, right now.'

'*Me?*' Georgina looked aghast.

'No need to be frightened. We can meet her magic with ours.' Lulah bent down and hugged Melissa, who had tottered over. 'I'll be back, but not before she's gone.'

'You have to carry me today,' Melissa warned them.

'Yes, cabbage, and we'll get the wind to push us along.'

'Are you sure she's coming, Lulah?' Georgina asked, feeling foolish.

'Sure is, Miss Georgie, I can feel it.' Lulah's thin frame was stretched to wire tautness. There was even a slight look of wildness about the huge black eyes under a mop of curly hair. 'Miss Lucinda brings trouble, like so many times in the past.'

'Then you'd better go, Lulah,' said Georgina. 'I thought this afternoon we might run out to the Ten Mile Lagoon. The children love it there.'

'Plenty of people are frightened of Miss Lucinda,' Lulah said. 'You can't see that light around her, miss?'

'I can sense an aura around her, Lulah,' Georgina

agreed, 'but I can't see any light. Only certain people have that gift.'

'*My* people,' said Lulah.

Less than ten minutes later, Lucinda arrived, and Tiger, who scarcely roused himself for visitors except to thump his tail, sprang to aggressive life and began to howl his hostility.

'What's wrong with Tiger?' Timmy hurtled into the parlour, still wearing his paper bag puppet on his hand. 'Oooh, look, Aunty, she's hitting Tiger with her whip!'

'*Timmy!*' Catching a child was the hardest thing of all, and Timmy, scarlet-faced, was too angry to respond.

'Dear God!' Unable to head either the dog or the child off, Georgina rushed out on to the verandah just in time to see Lucinda swish desperately at the leaping dog.

'*Tiger!*' Georgina shouted imperatively, and to back it up unleashed a piercing whistle, one not even her brother had been able to better. 'Come *here*!' She stamped the timber floorboards and Tiger miraculously broke off his clamour and tore up the steps, not coming to heel at Georgina's feet as she hoped, but racing onwards into the house like a runaway horse. 'Timmy, come and get Tiger and put him outside,' Georgina yelled. 'Don't cry, Missy, darling,' she said to her little niece, who was now racked with sobs. 'Damn it,' Georgina muttered, and picked Melissa up.

'If you ask me,' Lucinda fumed, coming up the stairs glaring-eyed, 'that dog needs to be put down!'

'For God's sake, Mrs Shieffield, he never even touched you!' Georgina said defiantly.

'It was plain he wanted to *eat* me!' Lucinda returned furiously. 'I feel compelled to speak to Quinn about the animal!'

'I'm sorry he barked at you,' Georgina said coldly. 'He's usually such a friendly dog.'

'Excuse me, my dear,' Lucinda said shortly, 'dingoes are *not* friendly.'

'No more than any other dog, I expect, depending on how they feel towards a certain person. We've had dogs all our lives, but even the tamest, most lovable dog can take a violent dislike here or there. Actually I think Tiger ran out to greet you when you met him with that whip.'

'I should think so—what else?' Lucinda shrugged her vicious sweeps aside. 'Every time I come here that child seems to be crying!' She glanced impatiently at Melissa, who was sobbing on Georgina's shoulder.

'For a very good reason,' Georgina answered pointedly. 'When she saw you whipping Tiger it scared her half to death.'

'If you ask me...' Timmy puffed into sight, still looking red and belligerent.

'No one asked you, darling,' Georgina headed him off firmly. 'Did you tie Tiger up?'

'No, I didn't. He's hurting like mad.'

'Rubbish!' Lucinda's coal black eyes narrowed dangerously. 'I used the whip to frighten him off. I didn't hurt him, I'm sure.'

'He's *bleeding*!' Timmy threw one terrible glance in Lucinda's direction, then he went to his aunt. 'Why don't we get Daddy home?' he wailed.

'And when he does come home he'd better pull you into line, young man. You're the rudest child I've ever met!'

'*Please*, Mrs Shieffield,' Georgina begged. 'I know you'll accept that Timmy is wound up like a top. The children are very attached to their pet.'

'Oh, do stop crying,' Lucinda snapped to Melissa. 'Why, I'd very much like to know, were they allowed that dog in the first place? A dingo, as bold as brass!'

'I did say I'd lock him away,' said Georgina. 'If only I knew when you were calling, Mrs Shieffield?'

'As it happens,' Lucinca sat down, 'you've been invited to Windarra for the weekend. You must have impressed our neighbours.'

'Why, how nice of them,' said Georgina. 'But of course, I have the children.'

'The Wintons have already decided the children are welcome. Beggars for punishment, I suppose.' Lucinda looked at Georgina with those strangely mesmeric eyes. 'Heard from your sister-in-law?'

'Not as yet. I've sent mail to her.' Georgina, too, sat down with Melissa, subsiding, on her knee.

'And what did it say?'

'What it was meant to say.' Georgina raised her head. 'We're all well but missing her. How much I love Rambulara.'

'Ah, yes, you love Rambulara, of course. It's just possible it wouldn't be quite so fascinating if Quinn wasn't here?'

'Certainly it wouldn't,' Georgina said humorously. 'He's such good copy as the big cattle baron.'

Lucinda gave her a long look. 'You can't mean you hope to put him in your magazine?'

So, as far as Lucinda knew, Georgina hadn't already asked him. 'The thought had crossed my mind.'

'My dear, you have no hope,' Lucinda said sneeringly. 'I daresay there are a few journalists around one could grant an interview, but not you.'

'And why not?' Georgina looked down to cut Timmy's comment off.

'You're too young, for one thing. A female. And your magazine simply isn't prestigious enough.'

'Going from back to front, *Profile* is emerging as one of the front runners, females make excellent interviewers—and I don't consider myself all that young. When one loses one's parents fairly early in life, it makes a big difference. From being the one who gets cared for you find yourself doing the caring. Your capacities are exploited early.'

'Yet your brother doesn't seem to have done much with his life?'

Georgina shook her head. 'I'm sure I don't know how you figured that out. He fell in love with the right girl, he married her, and now they have two beautiful, healthy children. He loves station life, and who knows, some time in the future he may be able to manage some property or find a small one of his own.'

'I almost believe you,' Lucinda answered lightly. 'But surely the marriage is unworkable? Rick has spoken to me from time to time.' There was the sheen of triumph in her fathomless eyes.

But Georgina's reply was very calm and neutral. 'Quite frankly, Mrs Shieffield, I doubt that. In any case, this is no time to discuss it.' Not with Melissa looking up at her and Timmy making snapping motions with his puppet.

'As you like,' Lucinda yawned delicately, hand before a bitter rosebud mouth. 'What do children really take in, anyway?'

'The lot, I assure you,' Georgina returned smartly. 'Was there any message that had to be returned to the Wintons?'

'Lord, let me see . . . I didn't take it, of course. The housekeeper did that. I believe Bob Winton is flying in for you—a very earnest, dull fellow, given to moralising. I recall years ago he very nearly accused me of sending my husband to his death.'

Georgina remained silent, while Lucinda's strangely flat black eyes looked into the past.

'But then, I'm afraid, a lot of self-righteous fools did that. I'm sure I had absolutely nothing to do with it. Tell me, Miss Hamilton, have you heard about my husband?'

'I was only told about his . . . accident.' Georgina set Melissa down on her feet and spoke to her nephew. 'Timmy, be a good boy and make a puppet for Melissa.'

'Want to glue the hair on,' said Melissa.

'Yes, Aunt.' Timmy rose to his feet, a handsome little boy, full of bright challenge. He looked at Lucinda and said coolly, 'Goodbye, Mrs Shieffield. I'm sorry I was rude. Tiger doesn't fancy you either.'

'I believe that boy is much brighter than his father,' Lucinda said surprisingly. 'You realise, of course that your brother is experiencing the most embarrassing crush on me?'

'First things first, Mrs Shieffield,' said Georgina. 'What happened to your husband?'

'My dear, you've heard. He was just killed! I grieved for almost a year, but David was always doing manic things. He had moods, you see—something in his biochemistry and always wanting to top his brother. Of course he never did—except to marry me. That was his greatest victory.'

'You mean he married you to upstage his brother?'

'Something like that.' Lucinda put a hand to the raven coil on her nape. 'Oh yes, he was madly, crazily in love with me. Both the boys were, from when we were children. But Quinn and I were always meant for each other. We were always fighting, always making up. Except for the time I threw his engagement ring at him. I told him I hated him. I was so angry it was *odd*. I love Quinn, I've always loved him, and I always will. That was the terrible source of poor David's dissatisfaction. I tried to be a good wife to him, but some relationships are irrevocably sealed. David really was never any more than Quinn's shadow. Even when he used to make love to me I made myself believe it was, in fact, Quinn.'

'How terrible!' Georgina murmured in dread. She wanted to hear no more of this, but Lucinda didn't even notice her or her agitation.

'Of course he never forgave me for marrying his brother,' Lucinda went on. 'Quinn never gives up what is his. Now he makes me suffer in unspeakable ways.' There was real anguish in the burning glance she turned on Georgina. 'He's going to make me crawl to him on bended knees!'

This was far indeed from what Georgina wanted to hear, but was it really so unexpected? Quinn Shieffield and Lucinda were capable of far crueller games than any she had ever played. Blessed with a sunny nature, Georgina could not bear to injure anyone, but she had allowed Quinn Shieffield to threaten her peace of mind. It had been easily managed, from the beginning.

'You look shocked!' Lucinda gave her sneering smile.

'I *am* shocked, Mrs Shieffield. But none of this has anything to do with me, and really, I'd rather not hear.'

Lucinda rolled her jet-black eyes. 'You're more like a doll than a real woman. Don't you have feelings behind that bouncy, schoolgirl manner?'

'Get this, Mrs Shieffield,' Georgina said shortly, 'I'm sufficiently bouncy not to allow *you* to bounce *me*. And furthermore, I admire a certain reserve. It's not necessary for you to tell me about your grand passion to keep me entertained.'

'Well, really!' Lucinda gave her a smile that was more like a glare. 'You're on Rambulara, my dear. You're really not free to say what you like.'

'Rubbish!' Georgina threw up her tawny head. 'You certainly throw away words as you like.'

'Ah, yes, but then I'm a Shieffield.'

'Did you ever hear about a democratic society?'

'Oh, tut!' Lucinda's little white teeth gleamed. 'I don't have the beginning of an idea what that means. The Shieffields have always lived like aristocrats.'

'Maybe so, but they come pretty close to ordinary people, which may be the source of their survival. It struck me that Mr Shieffield is a very egalitarian man. The people around here don't just obey him because he's the Boss. They admire and respect him. He has the natural authority of a born leader, but he works just as hard as his men.'

'Now isn't that nice?' Lucinda tilted her raven head, for all the world like a hawk. 'Maybe you've got a crush on Quinn yourself? Much good it would do you!'

'I'd prefer not to talk about my brother's employer,' Georgina said in a spirited voice. 'You don't mind if I take the children for a drive, do you?' As she asked her question, she pointedly stood up.

'Does it cause you a lot of bother, the thought that I could destroy your brother?' The complacency in Lucinda's voice was devastating.

Georgina shook her head. 'You can't do that, Mrs

Shieffield. Richard knows perfectly well you're only playing a game with him.'

'Maybe so, but I could have him if I wanted him,' Lucinda said incredibly.

'And why would you want him?' Georgina looked at her with naked disgust.

'Maybe now, to punish you. You're a fool if you think you can cross swords with me, Miss Hamilton. You're not in my league, make no mistake about that.'

'That wasn't necessary for you to tell me,' Georgina said. 'I could appeal to you not to break up my brother's marriage, to make his innocent wife and children suffer, but I know Rick has too much sense, too much honour, to betray the people he loves best. If you were a different sort of woman, if there was a real possibility that he could love you, I would be terribly worried—no, brokenhearted, but among other things we all know who fills your head and your heart.'

'And still your brother will be in my power,' Lucinda laughed. 'Go for your drive, Miss Hamilton. Take those good-for-nothing friends with all their stories of their blessed Dreamtime. Embrace it all while you can, because I assure you you'll very soon depart—you and the children. I'm sure you'll have to go all the way with them, look after them and their dreary little mother. At least she could accept what you can't. She's lost your brother. He's a romantic, a dreamer. He wants to fall madly in love with a sleeping princess.'

'If there were any around, it was a long time ago.' Georgina handed Lucinda the riding whip she had set down on a table. 'I very much regret we've had to speak of these shocking things, Mrs Shieffield. It seems somehow unreal.'

'It's real enough,' Lucinda laughed. 'Anyone can live life on your level, but in our world, Quinn's and mine, one never knows what might happen.'

Georgina shrugged and looked away. 'Thank you for delivering the message from the Wintons, but I don't think I'll be able to go.'

'Of course not, my dear.' Lucinda went down the steps, her mouth quivering with biting scorn. 'You're so scared you have to stay home and look after little brother.'

It was so true, Georgina realised, there wasn't a single thing she could add. She could just see Lucinda trapping Rick into peril. It would be like a snake with a little bird. Rick wouldn't want to be dishonourable, but Lucinda was a strange, disturbing woman, the sort of woman who could make the sanest man a little unhinged. Hadn't her enemies accused her of driving her husband into the unknown? The feelings she aroused in people were too powerful, too complex for Georgina to take in. Quinn Shieffield himself wasn't immune to her black magic; Georgina had seen the evidence of it in his face. Theirs was a strange, secret relationship, and now Georgina felt incredibly angry and humiliated with herself for her own weakness. It was quite simple, really. Lucinda was using Rick for her own means and Quinn Shieffield was using her. What had seemed so perfect was really very terrible.

Towards sunset, when the men were starting home, Georgina drove up to the house, for the first time unexpectedly intimidated by its shadow. Hers was the world of the working girl and the homestead was a place where rich people lived. Not rich, doing very comfortably, but rich enough to take the breath away. She had been told by Rick that recently the Shieffields had sold some shares worth about five or six million, and Rick had commented wryly that it was a mere drop in the ocean. The family assets were said to be enormous.

As Georgina neared the open doorway Edwina Shieffield emerged from the entrance hall, her sad little expression warming to life.

'Why, Miss Hamilton—Georgina!'

'How are you, Miss Edwina?' Georgina took the tiny hand that was held out to her. 'You mustn't think I was calling for no good reason . . .'

'I know why you're calling,' Edwina nodded emphatically. 'Bruce isn't calling for us as expected. Quinn will fly us over.'

'You mean you're going to Windarra?'

'Of course I'm going!' Edwina motioned her into a seat. 'Nell is a special friend of mine and I like young company as well.' She smiled at Georgina cheerfully. 'Don't tell me you don't want me, dear.'

Georgina's hands moved in an expressive gesture. 'I'd love to have your company, Miss Edwina. There's so much you can tell me, but I really don't feel I should leave Rick, and the children might be a little bit of bother for the Wintons.'

'Stuff and nonsense!' Edwina patted her hand. 'Your brother will be off some place anyhow. Do you suppose that hasn't occurred to Quinn?'

'I beg your pardon, Miss Edwina?' Georgina looked faintly embarrassed and startled.

Edwina fluttered a glance backwards towards the entrance hall, then winked at Georgina. 'You couldn't get up early enough to beat Quinn, so don't you go fretting. He'll put a lot of distance between Lucinda and that young man.'

'You mean my brother?' Georgina spoke quickly, her face flushing.

Edwina nodded her snowy head. 'Lucinda is just taking advantage of that boy. She's always trying to prove how fascinating she is—feeds on it like a drug. The one man she couldn't fascinate was Quinn.'

'She *must* have, for a time.' Despite herself the words jumped out.

'They were thrown together, my dear,' Edwina told her. 'Her mother never gave up on what she wanted, and neither does Lucinda. Why, half her tragedy is the way she was raised—so petted and pampered and pandered to, it destroyed all her character. She was a child who could have anything, do everything she pleased. In a way she had some terrible power over her own parents. A dangerous thing, power. Lucinda uses it in a sinister way.'

'Did I hear my name used?' a woman's voice said from behind them.

Aunt Edwina sat quite still looking before her, but Georgina whirled about. 'Good afternoon, Mrs Shieffield.'

Lucinda stared at her from head to toe, seemingly affronted by Georgina's effortless, inexpensive chic, and pronounced colour sense. This afternoon she was wearing a combination of marigold colours, light and dark, in a pair of culottes and a tiny camisole top, and she looked almost blazingly alive; the colours doing something astonishing to her eyes and her skin and her hair.

'Whatever are you doing here, Miss Hamilton?' she asked rudely.

'What does it look as if she's doing?' Aunt Edwina said serenely. 'She's talking to me.'

'Well!' Lucinda shrugged coldly. 'Don't let me keep you.'

'Sounds like you're going some place, Lucinda,' Aunt Edwina said sweetly.

'I'm going down to meet Quinn.' She swept past Georgina, ignoring her. 'I thought it was all settled, Miss Hamilton? You've come to look after the children. You should *do* it.'

'Sometimes, Lucinda,' Aunt Edwina exclaimed indignantly, 'you're beyond me!'

'I suppose so.' Lucinda gave the old lady a quick smile, but there was a mixture of anger and derision in her eyes. 'At any rate, I'm not completely fooled by Miss Hamilton.'

'I wish I knew what that meant,' said Georgina, trying to keep her reckless temper under control.

'I think, like your brother, you might deal in adventuring.'

'She certainly seems spunky enough,' Aunt Edwina said, and caught at Georgina's hand as though sensing her rising anger. 'You've been pretty adventurous yourself, Lucinda, at times—not to say alarming!'

'Quinn's coming now.' Georgina, caught up in a storm, used his christian name, and the way she used it revealed a degree of intimacy she had wished to hide.

Lucinda turned abruptly and stared at her. 'I don't think I care for such familiarity.'

'You don't think she's going to keep calling him Mr Shieffield, do you?' Aunt Edwina snorted in sudden amusement. 'You stick more to the old ways, Lucinda, than I do. Quinn. Mr Shieffield, who cares?'

'*I* do,' Lucinda returned shortly. 'Miss Hamilton has no position here. She's come to look after her brother's children, and her brother is a station hand, of all things!'

'He's young, strong, handsome, well mannered and well spoken. I thought you'd taken rather a shine to him, Lucinda,' said Aunt Edwina.

'How ridiculous, Aunt Edwina!' Lucinda's anger was terrible. 'I'm very glad you're always kept at home, otherwise you'd be saying these things in front of others.'

'I know. I must work harder to hold my tongue,' Aunt Edwina said dully. 'Quinn mustn't know I've made you angry.'

'Perhaps I should tell him,' Lucinda said viciously. Her eyes were narrowed to jet slits and her red, chiselled mouth sneered.

'Nothing *you* could ever say would be dreadful, Miss Edwina,' Georgina grasped the old lady's hand. 'Nothing. Not ever.'

'Please don't interfere, Miss Hamilton.' Lucinda ordered with extreme exasperation. 'Aunt Edwina is no more than a child. She speaks out like one.'

'Whereas you go in for the no-holds-barred. Miss Edwina is family, and when you come to think about it, you aren't,' Georgina retorted.

'That's right!' Aunt Edwina said smugly. 'I was always called Shieffield, but you're a Hallett, aren't you, Lucinda? And if you marry again you'll have another name.'

'Oh, do be quiet!' Lucinda snapped with a sob in her breath.

It was like a slap in the face to poor Aunt Edwina, and Georgina decided she wouldn't forgive or forget that. There was that childlike quality in Aunt Edwina that made one want to protect her, or rather, it made most people want to protect her. Lucinda looked as though she could push the old lady over a cliff, her heavy-lidded eyes glinting like black marbles.

Aunt Edwina clearly wanted to get up, and Georgina assisted her. 'We'll have a lovely time this weekend, I promise you,' she looked down at the old lady.

'So you're going now, are you?' Lucinda laughed. 'But . . . I thought . . .'

'It doesn't really matter what you thought, Mrs Shieffield,' Georgina spoke coolly.

'Steady, dear,' Aunt Edwina warned her, her blue eyes distressed. 'I can never tell which way Lucinda will turn. Even now.'

'Aunt Edwina has sense!' Lucinda said tersely. 'And she's known me for a very long time indeed.'

'I think I'll go inside and sit quietly,' Aunt Edwina said. 'I feel very old sometimes.' She patted Georgina's hand with several blind little motions, then wandered away through the open doorway.

'She's impossible these days,' Lucinda said balefully. 'Sometimes I think she's not responsible at all. It seems to me she'd be better off in a nursing home, but Quinn won't hear of it.'

'You mean you've talked to him about it?' Georgina asked, appalled.

'I talk to Quinn about—everything!' Lucinda told her.

'What an almighty cheek!' Georgina fired up, not caring. 'You can't really be that poisonous you'd want to put Miss Edwina in a home? Why, I should think it would kill her!'

'There is that,' Lucinda gave a weird gurgle. 'Let's say, anyway, it's my business. It's certainly not yours. Please remember that.'

The lone rider on horseback had now disappeared, heading towards the stables complex. Georgina crossed her arms almost protectively in front of her and moved past Lucinda, a feline creature in a black and ivory slip dress. If she hurried she could have a word with Quinn before he reached the house. Could Aunt Edwina really have heard Quinn intended sending Rick away from the compound? He was so sharp, after all, he probably realised Lucinda's shattering effect on her susceptible brother. Hadn't he loved her himself, once? Maybe he didn't love what she had become, but it would be difficult to forget the feel of her in his arms. Lucinda showed no warmth, no liking towards her own sex, but even Georgina had discovered her success with men was phenomenal. The women men seemed to like best were really not very correct and often not very nice.

Georgina was still sighing when she almost walked into Quinn Shieffield's arms.

'Hi, stranger,' he said briskly, 'what's the matter with you today?'

'Do I look as though something's wrong?' She lifted her eyes, blasted away by the force of his attraction; feeling sorry for herself and not knowing why.

'First, you're frowning,' he touched a finger to her forehead, 'and I could hear someone sighing as you were plunging through those trees.'

'I've got a problem,' she confessed.

'Well, it's not the way you look.'

She didn't want to fall deeper and deeper into those sapphire blue eyes. 'Did you say you would fly us over to Windarra? Me, the children, Aunt Edwina?'

'Does it cause you any inconvenience, Miss Hamilton?' His eyes touched her face and her hair and the line of her throat.

The fears inside her caused her to tremble a little. 'I really appreciate being asked,' she said simply, 'but I don't feel entirely happy leaving Rick on his own.'

'Come on, Georgina,' he said a little shortly, 'he's not a little boy.' He put out his hand and she almost jumped backwards to avoid it. 'Stop that, you little fool!' There was no mistaking the flash of anger in his eyes. 'Keep still, or you may find yourself with a nasty sting.'

'Oh, what *is* it?' she pleaded, coming to attention like a child.

'A rather disagreeable little insect. I would say it fell into your hair in dumb shock. Instead of all those flowers it expected, dahlias and chrysanthemums and the like, a whorling, silky web.'

'Have you got it?' Georgina stood there quietly, with bees circling a six-feet-high hedge covered in pink blossom.

'I expect something for that as well,' Quinn told her.

'Never again,' she said crisply.

'Your words, Georgina, not mine.' As he spoke, he tilted her head and she had the giddy feeling of being thrown backwards, mastered.

'Please, Quinn,' she said faintly. 'It can't be.' She seemed to be staring up at him an immense way; tall, black-haired, blue-eyed, dark golden skin, lean with wide shoulders, narrow-hipped, too damned beautiful.

'Forgive me if I'm disturbing you,' a savage voice called sweetly.

'That's your scene,' Quinn returned stingingly.

'I'm only trying to protect Miss Hamilton before she's ruined.'

'How kind of you, Mrs Shieffield.'

'Don't mention it.' There wasn't a vestige of colour in Lucinda's matt white skin. 'The number of women who've revolved hopelessly around Quinn!'

'So there you are, Georgina,' Quinn gave her a mocking, twisted smile, 'a supreme philanderer without knowing it.'

'Obviously that's what Mrs Shieffield would like me to believe, but you don't seem to fit. Possibly you're a one-woman man.'

'He is, and he hates it!' Lucinda laughed wildly.

Georgina shuddered and stepped away, but Quinn

caught her rather painfully by the shoulder. 'You wanted to speak to me about something, didn't you?'

'Yes, I did.' But she knew she couldn't find the words in front of Lucinda.

'I'm here. I'm waiting. Lucinda,' he turned to his sister-in-law, the hardness of his expression wounding, 'buzz off.'

'Watch how you speak to me, Quinn,' she protested.

'Now!'

He took his hand from Georgina's shoulder and made the slightest movement towards her, his lean body coiled like a leopard about to spring.

Then a shocking thing happened. Lucinda brought up her hands powerfully above her head, gave a kind of howling scream, then pivoted and whirled away.

'Dear God!' Georgina muttered, inadequately. She had the strong suspicion Lucinda Shieffield was unbalanced. Yet wasn't *he* fiercely cruel to her? 'I can't go to Windarra with you tomorrow—I just can't. I'm sorry to disappoint the Wintons and Miss Edwina, but they'll do perfectly well without me.'

'Come off it,' he said violently. 'You don't trust your fool brother, and I don't either.'

'You . . .' He made her so angry it was all she could do not to bring up her hand.

'Damn it, you nearly hit me!' His blue eyes, his dark formidability were tying her in knots.

'No.'

'It's true I've never hit a woman in my life, but I'm telling you, Georgina, I'd slap you.'

'Terrific!' The tears swam into her eyes.

'Don't do that,' he said in a toneless voice. 'You have a very strange effect on me, Georgina. I want to carry you off and flay you alive.'

She could not be unaware of the savage sexual current that was running between them. She was even half sobbing with its hopelessness. 'Oh, *please*, Quinn,' she begged, her amber-coloured eyes wet with tears.

'Stop it. I *mean* it.' He was absolutely serious.

'Okay.' She dipped her head, bit her lip and fought for control. 'Rick was married before he met many women. Certainly he's never met anyone like your sister-in-law in his life. He loves Jilly, but he can't stop himself from looking at Lucinda. She's so beautiful.'

'Is she?' Quinn lifted one black eyebrow, looking diabolical. 'I've missed it.'

'But you loved her. You were engaged to her.'

'I remember it vaguely. It was a long time ago.' He looked utterly cold and ruthless. 'Now set your mind at rest. Your brother won't be left at home to have a whale of a time. I'm sending him and two others up to the Territory for a few days. They can tackle a few jobs there.'

'Does he know?' The fears inside Georgina began to subside.

'He knows now. This is a working station, Miss Hamilton. Your brother is here to work if I have to reshape him with my own hands. You don't know how to do it, and you've had your chance. Your big-sister efforts are quite doomed. He won't learn to stand on his own two feet if you keep propping him up. He won't learn the hard moral lessons if you keep getting in the way. I know all about his little flutter with Lucy, I assure you. I've just tolerated it to give him the chance to pull out of it himself. In my opinion he was finding it a damned sight easier than you think.'

'Well, Jilly wasn't,' Georgina said angrily.

'*Women!*' he groaned.

'You positively said that contemptuously,' she fired.

'It was not an insult, Miss Hamilton,' he said wearily. 'More an exclamation of despair. Now, do you think you could turn yourself in the direction of your little bungalow? I don't know about the rest of you, but *I've* had a hard day.'

CHAPTER EIGHT

THE weekend on Windarra was a very pleasant interlude after all the high drama Rambulara had supplied. Bruce Winton was not a man for such things in any case, and neither was his family. Georgina was among her own kind of people, ordinary, nice, sane, sensitive souls, not those of more than life-size dimensions, seething with passions on an unmanageable scale. It was all very pleasant and social, with lots of talk and laughter. The Wintons did much, much more than Georgina, who preferred to store up all they told her for future reference. Finding out all she could about the Outback and its unique people was high up on her list of priorities, and anyone who has a good story to tell always likes to be encouraged. Georgina got all the co-operation that she needed, and Aunt Edwina, clearly enjoying herself, manoeuvred in lots of little anecdotes of her own, mostly whimsical but often more revealing than her family might have cared for. She was a very sweet and strange little lady, like someone out of a fantasy, but the Wintons had long since taken her to their hearts. Windarra was one of the few places where Aunt Edwina Shieffield felt free to go and where her hosts could be absolutely relied upon not to gossip about what she had said. Georgina supposed one could call Aunt Edwina eccentric. Vague she might be, given to unexpected asides and confidences, but her observations about people were uncannily penetrating and accurate, even a little scary.

'Never confront Lucinda on your own!' Aunt Edwina had told her, a few moments before she had closed her eyes that first night. Georgina had found herself acting more and more like a young, caring relative than a near-stranger, and she had settled the old lady for bed.

The warning had kept her fully awake for hours, to the extent that she slept later the next morning than she intended. Ruth Winton, in fact, had taken care of the children just as soon as they stirred, which was to say with the birds.

Windarra homestead was a very pleasant place; a large, rambling building of no particular design but fitting well into its high setting on a knoll. The house itself was drenched in bougainvillea and almost dwarfed by huge trees. Unlike Rambulara it wouldn't have thrilled a house-buff out of his socks, but the atmosphere was so mellow and comfortable it was almost like paradise while it lasted.

Quinn had flown them in, but Bruce Winton was to fly them home.

'You must come again, Georgina,' Ruth Winton told her, her face pink with pleasure. 'I don't think I've laughed so much in a long time. And don't forget to send us an autographed copy of *Profile* when the articles go in.'

'*If* they go in,' Georgina smiled.

'They will if you write as you talk.'

'I wannasitasideyou, Aunty,' Melissa pleaded.

'Say thank you to everyone for inviting you,' ordered Georgina.

'Thank you.' Melissa stepped towards Ruth Winton, arms up.

Timmy was holding the wonderful boomerang Bruce Winton had given him. 'I hope we're allowed to come again, Mr Winton?'

'Sure can, Timmy.' The big man ruffled his hair. 'Now, step lively, boy. I have to get you home before sundown.'

'Such fun!' Aunt Edwina said happily as they waved through the portholes. 'It's nice to escape from my own home.'

I'm going to do it, Georgina thought. I'm going to ask her what she means. But almost immediately the old lady's head fell back and she became engulfed in a pleasant doze.

Almost a week later, Rick returned, hurrying up the front steps and reaching for his son's small, flying body.

'Daddy!' Timmy cried in an ecstasy of love.

'How's my boy? Oh, Timmy, how I've missed you!'

'Rick!' Georgina surged towards her brother, clearly happy to have him home again.

'You want to know something, pal?' Rick grabbed her and hugged her. 'At least I know where I'm going now. Mick was forever showing me things, but I've suddenly caught on on my own. Nobody ever saw me put a foot wrong.'

'You liked it?'

'Loved it. Quinn's brother-in-law is a great bloke. And his sister is terrifically good-looking.'

'Really?'

'You can decide that for yourself. She's coming visiting soon.'

Something crashed over in the house, then as Georgina started forward, Melissa appeared, sleepy-eyed and adorable.

'Daddy, my Daddy! Have you brought Mummy home?'

'I'm going to do it,' said Rick. 'Damn it all, a family ought to be together,' he added fiercely.

'Perhaps you'd like to read what Jilly says in her latest letter,' Georgina offered.

'To *me*?' Rick's golden eyes blazed with hope.

'Not this time, little brother. You know what, I think you've grown inches.'

'Let's measure him,' suggested Timmy, his arms locked around his father's long leg. 'Aunty has been showing us magic, do you know that? She can make paper into flowers and birds. She can make them *fly*!'

'Got it all out of a book,' Georgina smiled. 'Oh, it's lovely to have you home, Rick. I've even made something I know you're going to love.'

'Chocolate cake,' Melissa twittered.

'You better come and say hello to Tiger, Daddy,'

Timmy exhorted. Tiger was indeed yapping noisily. 'Aunty found him a new collar that's just perfect.'

'I don't know what we'd do without Aunty,' said Rick, and stared around his family in turn. 'I'll go barmy if Jilly doesn't come home soon. You know, it's possible to get to manage a property on your own . . .'

They had a splendid tea, considerably earlier than usual as Rick professed himself starving, and there was Billy outside the door inviting them to another rainmaking ceremony.

'You go, Georgie,' Rick leaned back and stretched luxuriously. 'I'm bushed.'

'Can I go, Billy?' asked Timmy.

'As soon as your daddy says yes.'

'Me too!' Melissa rose to her feet.

'And leave me?' Rick looked at his little daughter incredulously. 'And who's going to look after your daddy, may I ask?'

Melissa faltered. She looked at Georgina, the waiting Billy and her brother, than she moved over to the circle of her father's arm. 'I'll look after you, 'til Mummy comes back.'

'That's my girl!' Rick actually had the grace to flush. 'What do you say if we write a letter to Mummy tonight? You can send her some of your art work.'

The ability of the aboriginal people to communicate with the spirits of rain and storms was a subject of fascination for the white people. The unfailing results of rainmaking ceremonies were uncommon, and one famous old tribal elder was justly famous or infamous for making floods. But for a long time now, though spectacular black clouds had built up in the sky and everyone's heart cried out for rain, not one drop had fallen.

'This time it's gunna *work*!' Billy told Georgina emphatically. 'I just hope we don't make a flood.'

The ceremony was already under way when Georgina and Timmy arrived, and they found their way around

the magic circle and sat down quietly on the rugs and
cushions they had brought. Although the days were
brilliantly hot and fine the desert nights could be
surprisingly cool.

'Right, darling?'

'Yes, Aunty.' Timmy's big eyes shone and the fires
threw a brilliant glow over his fascinated little face. The
outdoor life was wonderful for small boys, and this was
the outdoor life in its widest dimension. Georgina had
the feeling that scenes like this would have a binding
effect on her young nephew, the invisible bonds, strong
as steel, that kept the people of the Inland forever on
their land.

The drum and tap-sticks were calling. The blood-red
earth was vibrating with the pounding of a dozen feet.
It was Billy, Georgina realised, who was sending the
extraordinary sound of the didgeridoo far into the
night. For an instant she hadn't recognised him,
decorated as he was with paint and feathers and a very
spectacular necklet. This rainmaking ceremony was
productive magic, as were fertility rites or love magic.
There was protective magic as well, as in healing or
counteracting injury or accident and destructive magic
designed to bring sickness or death to those who had
dishonoured their tribe. Sometimes the rainmaking
ceremony could come into the destructive category,
destroying stock or crops, but Billy as the chief
scorcerer had only carried out beneficial magic for a
long time. There were rumours that once he had been a
dreaded *kurdaitcha* man who could curse or kill a
victim through the pointing bone, but Billy had never
spoken of such things. All he would admit to was being
the possessor of powerful magic, a specialist in the field
of sorcery. Georgina felt quite pleased she had him on
her side. There were too many cases of quite healthy
aboriginals lying down and dying when caught up in
black magic. So completely did they believe in these
ancient rites that once a bone had been pointed in the
unfortunate victim's direction, depending on the power

of the sorcerer and the susceptibility of the victim, the victim could be rendered extremely ill or die within three days. The Wintons had spoken of just such a case among the desert people. The victim's soul had been drawn into the bone, magic so powerful it had killed him outright.

As tonight's performance was not a sacred ceremony the women's attendance had been permitted. Now they were dancing in the background, their hand and arm movements elegant in the extreme. Singing and dancing played an important part in aboriginal communities, and the young children were allowed to join in; the boys with the men, the little girls with the women. One young girl about thirteen was dancing with a plump infant on her hip. The baby appeared to be enjoying itself enormously, its hand grasping a handful of the older child's curls.

'Isn't the baby funny?' Timmy whispered. 'He reminds me of the little kid on *Diff'rent Strokes*.'

'Same plump cheeks.'

'Do they keep doing this till the rain starts falling?' Timmy asked.

'I suppose they do on and off, but just to be certain, we'll keep saying our prayers,' Georgina told him.

A dainty little lubra walked around stoking the fires while the wheeling, crouching, leaping men kept up their chant. They were all accomplished dancers and the whole scene was weirdly haunting and effective.

'They must be singing to the Moon Man to help them. It seems such a long way off, hanging there in the sky. Such a big moon! When I'm a man I'll be able to go there.'

'Just imagine!' smiled Georgina, hugging him. Sometimes she was terribly afraid for the children of tomorrow; afraid for her own niece and nephew. Some important person in power had said Australia would be the safest place of all in the advent of a nuclear conflict, but could any place on earth be safe? Would the survivors want to keep on living?

Firelight outlined a man's tall shadow, and Timmy turned wonderingly towards it. 'Oh, it's you, Mr Shieffield?' He was already on his feet scrambling up the bank.

'I imagined you'd be home with your father.' Quinn took the child's hand.

'Aunty's here!' Timmy announced. 'Billy invited us to the rain dance, so we had to come.'

'I just hope Left-hand Billy hasn't lost all his old power. There was a time when he could rip off a storm at will.'

'Truly?' asked Timmy with as much delight as apprehension.

'One or two times things got right out of control. We were cut off for weeks.'

'Billy will make it rain,' the little boy said confidently. 'I know he will.'

Quinn Shieffield looked down at Georgina, sitting slim and curved upon the rug. 'You even manage to light up the mulga by night,' he said mockingly.

'That's exactly what a redhead is supposed to do.' She smiled at him and held up a hand for Timmy. 'Come and sit down, darling. We can't disturb the performance. All dancers are temperamental.'

'They're not going to throw boomerangs or anything?' Timmy made a dash for the rug.

'Not if we sit down.' Georgina moved over and made a place for Quinn on the rug. 'Do *you* think this is going to work?' she whispered.

'I'd hate to think it wasn't. The waiting and the hoping is driving us all crazy.' He sat down, lithe and relaxed, and Georgina could almost believe she felt relaxed too, until under the cover of darkness he linked his fingers through her hand.

She said nothing. She couldn't, with Timmy beside her, but she turned her glowing amber head and looked at him, excitement welling up in her stronger than the resistance and the vulnerability.

'Keep it up, Miss Hamilton,' he murmured. 'You're doing admirably.'

She tried a silent tussle, but it was quite impossible to break his loose but implacable grip. Of course if Timmy hadn't been there she wouldn't have allowed him to do this. The only thing she could do was sit stiffly, aware that he wasn't really watching the ritual, but studying the play of firelight on her defiant profile. He had to be aware of her leaping pulses, for now his thumb was searching the delicate tracery of veins in her wrist.

'Tormentor!' Involuntarily it broke from her.

'*What*, Aunty?' Timmy's upturned face betrayed his surprise.

'I thought they were quarrelling.'

Timmy smiled kindly. 'No Aunty, it's only a dance. I think what they're doing is trying to win over the gods.'

'So much for that!' Quinn laughed. 'Do sit still, Georgina. If you've any vague sense of grievance, think of what I'm doing for your brother.'

In the dark glade Timmy rolled over to lie on his stomach and Quinn moved back against a red gum, adjusting Georgina's body so she rested against him. It was like being pinned helpless.

'Honestly, your hair is like a flaring torch.' He tilted his head forward to look at her and his warm breath slid over her cheek.

'I don't know what's the matter with you!' She turned slightly towards him, the better to muffle her low, accusing tone, only the movement brought their faces closer together. There was a high-handed mastery in his rather amused expression and a sensuality that was deepening dangerously.

'Surely Timmy should be asleep by now?' he murmured smoothly.

'I think we *have* seen enough,' she said quickly.

'Oh, no, Aunty!' Timmy finally heard. 'We have nothing else to do, and this is exciting.'

'Hear, hear!' Quinn Shieffield seconded in an amused drawl. 'No need to rush away, Georgina. Stay exactly where you are.'

And so she did, with his hand resting lightly just inches from her breast. It was lovemaking by remote control, and utterly and completely devastating. The wind fluttered through the trees, causing all the little fires to crackle and blaze, and a night-hawk whistled from the gum just above them. It was a beautiful night and the moon shone with a soft brilliance over this world of sandhills and endless wilderness and the great stone desert.

The chanting that had started as a deep, low vibration was gathering force, an urgent throbbing that was echoed in the tension of Georgina's body. This must be giving Quinn's ego a tremendous boost, the trembling that was in her, and still he kept a firm hold on her so her nerves were stretched taut. Even in this poor season desert shrubs were blooming and in the clean air one had only to breathe to inhale myriad heady perfumes, broom-flower, boronia—she didn't know. She was too perturbed by her riotous feelings; the necessity to hold them in check. Her mind was a whole jumble of images; dancing natives, twenty fires, a white moon and the mushrooming trees. It wasn't a peaceful scene but progressively more stirring, a mesh of primitive magic and the incandescence of the bush; a heart that was slamming against her ribs, sensations that were too agitated to be pleasurable. She had never felt or expected to feel a sexual urgency that was staggering. She wanted to tip her head back just a little so she could feel his mouth come over hers. She wanted him to move his hand...oh, so much!

'Too bad you didn't come on your own,' he muttered, right against her ear, and just for a second, a mere second, his hand did come up and cup her breast.

The desire and the fear in her made her arch her back and release a plaintive, half-lost little moan. She wished she had never met him, but it was too late now.

'Me too!' Timmy, who was lying propped up with his chin in his hands, looked back and called. 'Let me hold on to your hand, Aunty.' It was obvious he had taken

Georgina's little moan as an expression of pleasurable excitement at the climaxing dance. 'I'm awfully pleased we're here,' he whispered happily. 'I expect it'll start to pour any day now!'

And pour it did.

The first rain originated from a monsoonal low over the Territory. The initial disturbance formed over the Gulf of Carpentaria, moved westwards across the Northern Territory, then curved back over Alice Springs, causing water to surge down the usually dry bed of the Todd River. The flash-flood turned into a torrent. The river banks were broken and one of the driest spots on earth was incredibly flooded out. The town was inundated and three people were drowned; two of them campers in the dry river bed that had not had water running through it for thirty years.

And all this exactly four days before the Prince and Princess of Wales with their twenty-three-member entourage were to arrive in Australia at the Alice Springs terminal. With such a grand event due to take place the people of the Alice had worked mightily to polish up their town, now the floods had presented them with a seemingly impossible task. The main bridge was out, cutting the town in two, the very finest accommodation set aside for the Royal couple inaccessible, and the extent of the clean-up operation daunting even for a people who worked very hard.

And what of the proposed trip? No one on Rambulara had intended to miss out on the great day, and even Lucinda had condescended to crush into the Super King Air. Some of the men were even driving; those that couldn't fit into the helicopter. Now everything seemed changed. Three oil men had been reported missing when their four-wheel-drive was swept away by a flooded creek. If the rain kept up, it would be impossible to get through.

But in the midst of it was *jubilation*. This was how the drought would break. The huge rain system that had flooded across the North and reached Alice Springs might not be a freak. The indications were the terrible drought that had blighted the nation could officially break within a few weeks. The desiccated Inland would flower again, the land would become productive, and Georgina hoped that now she would be able to see the glory the Outback poets spoke of when the vast, widening plains wore a thick carpet of wildflowers; mighty vistas that ran on to the horizon. She had heard that such spectacles were so breathtaking, so uniquely bizarre for these dry, arid areas that even hardened tourists just sat down and cried. And what was good enough for a much-travelled tourist was good enough for her too.

'Do you suppose we're *really* going?' she asked Rick at a dawn breakfast.

'You might, I don't know about me. This rain is a great enough blessing. They tell me the cattlemen are going mad with joy where it's fallen, but it sure messes things up. The fact is our soils, unlike those of Europe and North America, are so ancient they have shallow surface layers. In other parts of the world the fertile land is several metres deep, but you've only got to try to push a spade fifteen centimetres into one of our paddocks to strike subsoil. The rain doesn't soak in, it runs off, and the erosion is terrible. Why do you think the Boss has had all those scientist blokes out? The Shieffields pioneered this country, and I guess they have the obligation to resolve the conflict between two needs—to work the land and to stop erosion. Other properties get ravaged, but not Rambulara, even in the worst times. We don't go in for over-grazing either. That's caused a tremendous amount of sheet erosion. So you see the rain is our greatest friend and our greatest enemy too. I suppose you could fairly say it's either a drought or a flood and precious little in between.'

'What does the forecast say?' Georgina asked, and set down a huge plateful of steak and eggs before him.

'Rain Southern Queensland. Some showers starting to fall on the New South Wales border. Don't worry, darlin', we've been praying for rain and we're going to finish up praying for it to stop!'

As a prediction it seemed likely. Georgina vividly remembered the great flood of '74 when torrential rain nearly put Brisbane under water in the space of the Australia Day weekend. And even then all she and Rick had worried about was their little family of koalas in the huge gum trees in the back yard.

Later on in the morning Lulah brought her a message to have morning tea with Miss Edwina.

'I suppose she wants to talk about your trip.' Lulah smiled shyly. 'If I made a little posy for the Princess, do you think you could give it to her?'

'I can certainly try. Or better yet, give it to Melissa to present it for all of us. It's well known that Princess Diana loves children.'

Up at the homestead Aunt Edwina was as excited as a child. In fact, she greeted Georgina with an eager hug and a kiss on the cheek. 'Well, it's *on!*' she exclaimed excitedly, the pleasure she was feeling lending her face a curious illusion of youthfulness. 'Quinn has made all the arrangements and we fly in Saturday afternoon. They're all cleaning up as best they can, and there's been little change at Keith's place. Keith Bracknell—he owns Marawalla Station. I was surprised he didn't let the Prince and Princess have it, but it might have been too far out, or security or something. I've known Keith since he was a boy. He and Quinn used to undertake some daring adventures, I can tell you!'

'And it's all right to bring the children?' asked Georgina.

'Of course it's all right. After all, our young Princess is absolutely charming to children. I'm sure they'll both love to see all the children there. I think it's absolutely essential we all stick together. I'm not terribly keen on that Republic bit. I suppose I might see things through different eyes. The old world, I mean. My own dear

father used to call us "improved Poms".' Aunt Edwina
broke off and gave a delighted giggle. 'Poms who are
born in Australia.'

'So that's what it means!' Georgina smiled back into
the curiously innocent blue eyes. 'Anyway, we're
cousins at least considering more than eighty-five
per cent of us are of British stock. I'm certain the
Prince won't find any change in this country. I was in
the Brisbane Mall when the Queen went for her
famous walk. I was there at the Commonwealth
Games. I know the Queen feels happy and safe in
Australia.'

'Oh, goodness me, yes.' Aunt Edwina lay back in her
winged chair and wiggled her toes. 'I don't know
whether you know, but my mother was presented at
Court. She was a great beauty, you know . . .'

Aunt Edwina launched happily into her story, while
the kind and pleasant Edith Young, Rambulara's
housekeeper, served a delicious morning tea. Mrs Louis
Shieffield, Georgina had noticed, kept very much to
herself, and mercifully there was no sign of Lucinda.
When they had finished tea Aunt Edwina invited
Georgina into the library so she could look through the
magnificent Shieffield collection.

'It's considered to be one of the finest private
collections in the country,' Aunt Edwina told Georgina
proudly. 'The Shieffields have always been men of
education and exceptional intelligence.'

'Presumably that applies to the women as well?'
Georgina added playfully.

'Well, that didn't happen in my case, did it, dear?
Not everyone has been as nice to me as you are.'

'But Aunt Edwina,' Georgina laid a hand on the old
lady's arm, 'whatever do you mean?

'Don't worry . . . don't worry . . .' Aunt Edwina
murmured almost to herself. 'Papa did tell me I had one
great talent. I could look into a person's soul.'

'Well then . . .'

'But I was never quite like anybody else. Can you

imagine, when I was a girl, they used to describe me as a butterfly?'

'You're still very pretty, Aunt Edwina,' Georgina said firmly and really the old lady *was* enchanting.

'Now you have a look around on your own,' Aunt Edwina said in a breathless rush. 'I can see you're a girl who loves books.'

'Oh, I do!' Georgina stared up at the booklined walls, admiring the richness of the leather binding.

'Then this will be a veritable paradise for you!'

Left on her own, Georgina went along the shelves, pausing now and then to pick up a beautifully bound volume. She loved books much as a porcelain collector loves porcelain, and these jewelled covers were magnificent.

Georgina was just about to move across to the circular drum table and sit down when she caught the sound of Lucinda's distinctive voice. She was speaking to someone, a staff member by the sharpness, and Georgina obeyed her overwhelming desire to duck for cover. Far over by the window was a huge winged-back chair that would most certainly give her shelter. Lucinda would very probably go by, no doubt for her morning ride, so there was no real need to invite a resentful scene. Lucinda had already implied that Georgina was making an all-out effort to ingratiate herself with an old lady who was 'as mad as a hatter', not seeing, even if it were true, which of course it wasn't, that her own attitude towards Aunt Edwina was far more chilling. There seemed to be no sympathy in Lucinda at all, no humour or compassion. No pity for Jilly, who had retreated, beaten, before her contemptuous power.

Hidden away in the great armchair Georgina drew her slender legs under her. This chair must have been designed for a big man who liked a lot of comfort. It was positively swallowing her. All of which made her happy. Lucinda had a habit of riding; joining Quinn, waylaying Rick, if you like. In a few moments, very likely, she would be out of the house.

Yet the footsteps slowed and stopped, deepening Georgina's unease. She did not want to move, but she supposed she would have to. How was it possible that such a beautiful woman could repel people? It was as though the sinister cast of Lucinda's mind overpowered her undeniable physical beauty.

'Drat Lucinda!' Georgina thought, halfway decided to pull up out of the chair. It seemed so ridiculous to be hiding. Aunt Edwina had given her permission to use the library, after all.

Lucinda's voice came again, and this time the sound was thrilling. 'Quinn!' she called, just a little below normal level.

The sound of a man's footsteps coming along the corridor and then Quinn speaking, firmly to the point of sternness. 'For God's sake, Lucy, what is it this time?'

'There's something I must tell you. I can't put it off a moment longer.'

'You're getting married again, are you?' His voice was full of a sort of cruelty, and Georgina's embarrassment changed to a stricken panic. There was a taste of bitterness in her mouth, humiliation and dishonour. She couldn't bear to overhear what might happen now, not for their sake but for her own. No matter how much he denied it, Quinn could never forget he had been Lucinda's lover. *Had* been? Had he ever renounced her body? Georgina began to shake so badly she couldn't get up.

'*Please*, darling!'

Lucinda must have gone to him, for now they had both come into the room.

'You've got about two minutes, Lucy. Go ahead.'

'You're killing me, Quinn,' Lucinda vowed.

'Don't you ever talk about anything but yourself?' Quinn retorted curtly. 'Why don't you go home to your own people?'

'They don't want me,' she pouted.

'No, they think you're intolerable and always refuse

to take the blame. You were over-indulged and self-indulgent since childhood. You offend every damned person who comes near you. The house girls are terrified of you, and even Jennifer balks at your company.'

'You bastard!' Lucinda hissed. '*You* made me what I am!'

'No, my dear, I did not.'

It was said so acidly that even Georgina stifled a sharp gasp.

'You don't truly believe that,' Lucinda moaned. 'You still love me, Quinn, but you dare not show it.'

'Almighty God!' Quinn grated violently. 'What did I ever do to deserve this obsession?'

'You transformed me when I was just a girl. For me, you were everything, all I'd ever dreamed about. David was a poor ghost beside you.'

'Don't speak my brother's name!'

The tone was so terrible Georgina wanted to put her head down and weep.

'You *make* me,' Lucinda cried. 'You blame me for David, don't you?'

'Then. And now.'

'Aah!' Lucinda made a sound like a suppressed cry of torture. 'You don't feel *any* responsibility?'

'The only way I could have stopped him from marrying you was by marrying you myself. And I would have done it had I known.'

'Because you loved me!' There was a sound of a movement, and Georgina had the bedevilled picture of Lucinda in Quinn's hating-loving arms. 'I was your first love, Quinn. Have you forgotten? You were drunk on loving me the night we became engaged.'

'I was certainly drunk,' he said dryly. 'Each of you, you and your mother, possessed extraordinary powers of persuasion. For all my flings I'd been brought up very conventionally, you know. After you conned me into seducing you I thought the least I could do was marry you.'

'You're lying!'

'Look, I don't like this, Lucy,' Quinn said impatiently. 'In my mind you're my brother's widow. Is that clear?'

'Because you've got a guilt complex you can't live with?' Lucinda cried. 'You want me, but you don't feel free to take me.'

'God, this is obscene!' Quinn groaned in the same terrible voice.

'Obscene, incestuous.' Lucinda laughed wildly. 'Oh, please, please, *please*, Quinn, don't keep punishing me for what happened to David. You know yourself he was far too reckless, inspired to prove he was better at something than you.'

'Let it drop, Lucy,' Quinn said tiredly. 'I want to remember my brother before *you* made his life a misery.'

'He loved me,' Lucinda insisted.

'Love? I think what he felt for you soon became the other side. You meant to make me unhappy marrying David, but the plan didn't work at all. Something quite unexpected had happened. I simply didn't care.'

'My God, you told yourself you didn't care. Then when David killed himself you turned to persecuting me. It's all been one long nightmare. Sometimes I think you want to drive me out of my mind!'

'I'd be very happy to drive you out of my house,' Quinn said cruelly. 'I swear while you're here there's a bloody curse on it. You've got to decide, Lucinda, what you want to do with your life. What there is of our relationship is only destructive. You have all the money you could possibly need. I think it's time you found yourself a place of your own. God knows I've been generous enough.'

'I suppose it's that girl,' Lucinda exclaimed suddenly, blazingly.

'Oh, hell, I can't stand this!' he muttered.

'Oh yes, you'll turn away, but it's no good, Quinn,' Lucinda cried dementedly. 'You must leave her alone!'

'And *you* must leave her out of it,' he snapped out

metallically. 'She has nothing whatever to do with you and me.'

'The colour of her hair—I *hate* it!'

'God, I know that. She knows that. We *all* know it. You're crazy, Lucy, and that's God's truth.'

In her armchair Georgina felt half frozen with horror.

'Then you'll have to be careful, won't you?' Lucinda was saying slowly. 'If you don't want me, you can't have anyone.'

'I should worry,' Quinn jerked out with obvious scorn. 'Just give me the slightest excuse and I'll have you put away for your own protection.'

'Words!' Lucinda shouted. 'Just words! We're bound together, Quinn, in the one prison.'

She must have hurried away immediately, because her booted feet thudded along the flight of carpet and clattered across the marbled entrance hall. If she was about to go for her morning ride, she could very well break her neck.

Georgina was afraid to stir, uncertain whether Quinn was still in the room or not, but the muscles in one of her legs were cramped and she eased her body very, very slightly.

'Who's there?' he whipped out so menacingly she could feel all the spirit and courage flowing out of her.

He was close to her now, then he was pulling her to her feet. 'What the hell!' he muttered.

The cramp in her right leg was so bad she was close to falling. Certainly she would have doubled over, only he was holding her wrists.

'Am I right in thinking you want a good story?' A blazing anger was in his jewel-bright eyes.

'I was trapped here,' she tried to explain, her face pale with distress and anxiety.

'What do you mean, trapped?' He was hurting her.

'Dammit, just what I said!' Her spirit was returning to her. 'Aunt Edwina allowed me to look over the library and I heard Mrs Shieffield coming, so I ducked.'

'You mean you hid?'

'Yes, I *hid*.' Was the blood ever going to flow through her leg again?

'What the hell's the matter?' Quinn asked fiercely.

'I've got a cramp,' she told him with a soft, hissing sigh.

'I should think you would.' He dropped her hands and pushed her back into the armchair. 'Which leg?'

'I can do it!' Her voice and her eyes blazed.

'Oh, shut up. It'll be the day when fool women tell me what to do and how to do it!'

'Not *this* one!' Georgina protested with a little sob. 'I can't wait to get away from here.'

His hand gripped her ankle, came up over the calf and in a series of small manipulations untied the muscles.

'Oh, that's better!' She could feel a few tears glistening in her eyes. 'I wanted to put my hands over my ears. I didn't want to listen—you must believe me.'

'You didn't have the guts to yell that you were there?'

'I've got plenty of guts,' she said fiercely, and a tear dropped on to his hand. 'But sometimes discretion is preferable to acts of heroism. *I* think your sister-in-law is unbalanced.'

'No question.' The peculiar whiteness was disappearing from around his nostrils. 'I've considered it my duty to protect her, but I'm afraid she's dragging us all down to an early grave.'

'*Did* you love her?' Without even thinking Georgina made him look at her by cupping her hands to his face.

'Georgina——' Clearly she had taken him by surprise.

'I know I have no right to speak of any of this, but I hate to see so much unhappiness,' she told him. 'This thing goes so deep with her and I can understand.'

'You couldn't be more different from Lucinda if you tried,' Quinn assured her.

'I'm talking about loving *one* man.' Her voice was

very soft and husky. 'That's what it comes down to, doesn't it? She's never forgotten.'

'She gives me the willies.' He tried for a taut smile, but there was no lightness in his eyes. 'Lucy and I have known each other all our lives. I know exactly how she ticks. *You* don't.'

'And you don't intend to answer my question?'

'Your question has no meaning. Lucinda is my brother's widow.'

'And you'll never marry her?'

'Never.' His tone was cold but with tremendous depth to it. 'Besides, I'd rather talk about you. What would happen, do you think, if I kept you my prisoner?' Now his arms came out, holding her to the chair.

Her topaz eyes were inordinately expressive, but she shook her head, afraid to answer.

'Was it very painful, what you heard?'

'I guess it was.' Now her long eyelashes touched her cheeks. 'I have a colleague in the office who always says men are more trouble than they're worth. I used to laugh at her, but now I'm not so sure.'

'You mean *I'm* trouble.'

'Of course you are.' The colour swept into her creamy skin. 'I feel like the proverbial moth done to a crisp by a flame.'

'But you think I only mean you—well, harm?'

'No.' Georgina was acutely aware of the pride in his eyes. 'I know what you are, so you needn't get ready to slash me to ribbons. I only mean I'm deeply attracted to you. We both know it, so it's just as well to have it out in the open. But I'll be going home soon and I don't intend to get murdered before I go.'

'Don't be so stupid,' Quinn said heavily.

'Not so stupid, really. Crimes of passion are happening all the time.'

'Is there anything here in this library I have to thank for that?' He stared around at the bookshelves. 'I know Aunt Edwina is very fond of Gothic novels.'

'All right, I'm a coward, then.' Georgina took a deep, fluttering breath.

'Much good it will do you.' He lifted her head up. 'You can't stand on the outside of strong emotions all your life. You're a passionate woman, Georgina, and that's what terrifies you most of all. Not poor Lucinda, who's running out of control. Not me. But you. You're like a frightened little girl holding out on yourself.'

'So what do you think I ought to do?' she whispered hoarsely.

'Find out what it really means, this feeling we have for one another.'

'I can't!' she sighed.

'Calm down,' he said.

'And what do you think you're going to do about Lucinda? God, you could be using me to block her out for all I know!'

'What is it about feelings that make people lose all their intelligence?' Quinn said tersely. 'I am *not* using you to block out anyone, as you so pathetically put it. I didn't think beautiful girls needed any back-up on confidence—but you're distressingly without vanity. Try a little natural self-complacency instead.'

'It's easy enough to fob me off with words,' she murmured, finding little joy in what he had said.

'I daren't think of anything else,' he said mockingly, 'there's always someone at the door. Unless . . .'

'Why, what is it?' She cried out convulsively because he was bearing her off to the fireplace, the open hearth in summer filled with a profusion of luxuriant plants.

'Easy!' he fended off her defensive little blow. 'You're going to enjoy this.'

'It would be much easier if you'd tell me what you were doing,' she told him.

Quinn didn't even bother to answer but folded his arms around her, and suddenly a whole section of the booklined wall was moving.

'Oh, my goodness!' Instantly she was in another world with no idea what to do next. With such an

ingenious inbuilt device one might have thought Aunt
Edwina would have alluded to it in one of their long
conversations. Aunt Edwina delighted in tricks, but she
had never so much as hinted.

Now they were in a small, unfurnished, windowless
room little bigger than a wide corridor.

'Hey, let's do that again,' she said shakily.

'We will in a moment.' The booklined wall continued
its circuit. 'Do you know how many of these there are
in the house?'

'One's enough.' Georgina tilted her head and stared
around her. 'Though I guess every house needs one.'

'You know how it is when someone uninvited
arrives.' His dark head came down over hers. 'Still trust
me?'

'Too bad I don't trust myself.'

'It's okay, Georgina. I only want to prove something.'

'You're going to break my bones,' she whispered.

'Sorry.' Very slightly he slackened his tight hold. 'Do
you know, I think you've got skinnier?'

'Where?'

He laughed out loud. 'Oh, Georgina! I can't really
tell you, you'd have to take off your clothes.'

Her mouth trembled and immediately he pinned it
under is own.

'*Quinn*,' she breathed into his mouth. What was it
about him that so altered her world? When she was in
his arms every natural consideration was set aside; their
social differences, family complications, the absurdity
of falling in love with him at once.

'We could stay here all day,' he murmured, tilting her
head back against his arm, 'only there isn't much air.
Probably we won't even need it.'

'Quinn ...' Rather dazedly she opened her eyes.

'Careful ... let's conserve what we've got.'

He was kissing her again, and suddenly the empty
room was filled with fireworks, an explosion of dazzling
lights.

'You have the most beautiful skin. I'd like to kiss every part of it.' His mouth was moving along her throat. 'Have you ever slept with anyone, Georgina?'

'That's my business,' she half-pleaded.

'Tell me—please!' he whispered.

'No. I've always been terrified of making the wrong choice.'

'You're going to sleep with me,' he told her softly.

'I *won't*!' she protested.

'Of course you will. Listen, we have a tunnel.' Now he started to do what she both longed for and feared, his fingertips making delicate, feathery circles around the tips of her breasts.

'Oh, don't do that, Quinn.' It was increasing her hunger for him at an alarming rate.

'Do you think you could get out of that shirt?' he suggested.

'No!'

'Right—well, I'll have to move in.'

She was wearing the lightest, front-clipped bra and after a moment of sudden, shocked withdrawal, she accepted his hand.

'You're like a little girl,' Quinn said quietly. 'I won't hurt you, Georgina. I'm only caressing your breasts.'

The pleasure was so intense it was suffocating, or else the air in the room was being quickly used up.

'Tell me what's happening to you?' he asked her, with a kind of gentleness she hitherto had not associated with him. Her breasts were naked, intensely pretty, the pink nipples erect, so sensitive to stimulation, pleasure was shooting through her like lightning. 'Come here to me.' He lifted her so that she fell against him and his mouth closed over her aching breast.

She seemed to be falling backwards, gasping, the excitement too strong for her. Past experiences had allowed her to stay firmly on course, but Quinn was the only thing in this world. What he wanted ... she wanted. She wasn't content with this, yet her body was so immensely fevered she was breathing so rapidly she was gasping. Gasping his name . . .

'It's all right, darling.' His voice seemed to come from a long way off.

'Quinn?' She *did* sound like a little girl.

'Hush!' He was smoothing the silky fabric of her bra over her breast.

'Is it airless in here?' she asked.

'No. It just feels like that,' he said wryly. 'Do you still believe I'm mixing you up with anyone else?'

'No. I expect I'm the only girl you've ever known who nearly flaked out.'

'Because you're very highly strung and you're what I want.'

'Am I?' She put a staying hand on his chest.

'Don't I look deadly serious?' he asked.

'You do.'

'Let's just say you had no chance from day one.'

She was startled and looked it, but the tautness of Quinn's expression didn't soften, neither did the glitter in his sapphire eyes. Only the hint of a smile played around his lips. 'You're just a baby, aren't you, Georgina?'

'I know there's a big difference between us,' she answered unhappily.

'Maybe,' he put his arm around her and kissed her cheek. 'But not enough to worry about. Now I think it's time for us to go back to that angry old world out there. God knows that was Paradise—and I mean it!'

CHAPTER NINE

SUNDAY, March 20, 1983, and the airport at Alice Springs was a sea of flags.

'Oh, I'm so excited, I think I'm going to *burst!*' moaned Timmy.

The sunshine was brilliant and all the townsfolk, the tourists, the Outback people who had arrived for this historic occasion were buzzing with Timmy's excitement and a very real pleasure. Prince Charles had always been tremendously popular in Australia and had visited it so often he could afford to be lighthearted, but it was reasonable to expect that the intensive Royal tour programmes might seem a little daunting to his beautiful young wife. The Royals were reared to handling huge crowds and eternal receptions, but the Princess, very naturally, might be a little nervous of such things. This was her first big tour, but so far as everyone at Alice Springs was concerned she might just as well learn to relax early, because she was about to be loved.

'That's them. They're here!'

'*Is* it?' Timmy demanded of his father.

'Certainly is, chum.' Richard swept up his son and perched him on his shoulder.

There was a great burst of clapping and cheering and the sea of flags began to wave.

Melissa, wearing her very prettiest pink dress with a matching pink bow in her hair, thought she had better cry.

'Darling, what is it?' Georgina had been hugging the little girl as she rested back against her, now she bent down to Melissa's level.

'I don't like my white socks,' the little girl whispered.

'They're lovely. I'll bet Princess Diana is wearing

something white—probably her shoes and bag. It looks
so lovely and cool and summery.'

'Will she be wearing pink?'

'We'll soon know. Now stop crying, pet. Remember
you must greet them with a *smiling* face.'

Melissa didn't cry again.

The RAAF B707 jet came in low over the gnarled
and twisted MacDonnell Ranges, like Ayers Rock and
the ancient domes of the Olgas, said to be the oldest
geological formations on earth, and touched down at
exactly seven-forty-eight a.m. to a great, reverberating
cheer. There was a crowd of about two thousand
assembled and what seemed like a tremendous battery
of photographers and reporters, including two of
Georgina's senior colleagues at *Profile* magazine.
Marion had in fact reported that Max was extremely
pleased with an article Georgina had already forwarded
and was waiting for more.

'Shouldn't be surprised if it gets in,' Marion had
added kindly. Privately Georgina had always considered
the older woman to be rather bitchy, but perhaps she
too was being warmed by the atmosphere.

Another great burst of cheering and clapping and
Prince Charles and Princess Diana appeared. The
Princess was wearing an exquisitely soft shade of
aquamarine and the white shoes Georgina had
predicted, much to Melissa's delight, and Prince Charles,
looking very relaxed, wore what the men called 'his
Territory gear'. Whatever it was, he looked good, and
his lady looked exquisite.

Prince William, who had cried only twice on the long
thirty-hour flight, was carried down to the tarmac by
his nanny, his soft blond hair glinting in the strong
sunlight.

'He's starting early,' Rick chuckled. 'He looks
thoroughly used to it already!'

And the little Prince did pose quite calmly for his
photograph, while his mother looked slightly tearful at
parting with her beloved baby for the best part of three

days, and Prince Charles, looking amused and indulgent, shooed away the nosey fly that was attempting to land on his son's golden head. Prince William was off to Woomargama Station where he was to stay while his parents toured the country.

It was a good start to a tour that was to turn into a triumph for to immensely likeable young people who had onerous roles to play; to keep the monarchy alive and hold the peoples of the Commonwealth together. Prince Charles was already superb at it, and the shy and trembling young woman who had started the tour was to make tremendous gains every day as the whole of the country was to observe and the press of the world record. Here were a people who weren't about to make her nervous, but delighted to meet her. Their warmth and friendliness worked its own magic.

The weather continued sizzling, turning a creamy English rose a decided pink, and Georgina and Rick and the children dashed around all the places where they could catch another glimpse of a very eye-catching couple.

'I think Pwince Charles is very handsome,' Melissa announced.

'Handsomer than me?' Rick feigned hurt.

'You're taller, Daddy, and you have a beard.'

'Sounds like I ought to shave it off!'

'Why don't you?' said Georgina. 'Certainly before Jilly gets back.'

The Alice Springs School of the Air produced far and away the liveliest session, with the children of the Outback plying the Royal couple with all sorts of questions and, unlike the madly jealous press, getting lovely, direct answers.

These children were spread over one and a half million square kilometres of the southern half of the Territory, and they had the most wonderful time asking questions about Prince William, his toys, whether he had a little bike and a pony, how many rooms there were in Buckingham Palace (a 'terrible question' for Prince

Charles), did the Prince cook a barbecue for visitors (Prince Philip took the honours).

Questions and answers, and it was hard to tell which were the more entertaining. Georgina found herself jotting it all down as much for her own records as anything else. Trust the children to get such marvellous stuff!

Meet the Press. Meet the children. Meet the Yankuncjatjara people, the tribe who called Uluru, Ayers Rock, their own. Prince Charles and Princess Diana drove right out to the base of the Rock to meet the white-bearded tribal elder, a famous tracker and hunter. Prince Charles was chief of his peoples, Naninga just as much a chief to the aboriginals grouped around him.

'It's going to take me a while to recover,' Georgina announced on that last day before the Royal couple flew off to Canberra. 'It just goes to show how exhausting these tours must be. All I've done is run around, ask a few questons and watch.'

'Think you've got enough for your article?' Rick drained down a cold beer.

'Tons.' She lay back in her planter's chair. 'I think Missy might sleep for a week.'

'Awfully nice of the boss to let me come,' said Rick.

'Awfully nice of Mr Bracknell to let us have this bungalow. I prefer it really to staying up at the house. Quinn's aunt and uncle can be very distant, and Lucinda is just terrible.'

'I suppose she is—*terrible*.' Rick admitted.

'My darling brother, keep telling yourself that every day. Every minute, every hour.'

'I never see her,' Rick said.

'Do you want to? Wait—tell me.' Georgina leaned forward and grasped her brother's wrist. She was staring intently into his face and she saw his golden eyes darken.

'It's silly, I know,' he agreed.

'You *want* to!' Georgina exclaimed in alarm.

'Oh, God, no.' Rick broke away and poured himself another beer. 'Why would I want to feel wretched when I think I've made Jill understand she has to come back to me?'

'You've told her you love her.'

'I *do* love her,' Rick said grimly. 'I had no idea she could be so furiously jealous. Little soft Jilly. Honestly, it was like a madness.'

'It was a madness all right, and *you* had it,' said Georgina sternly.

'Not any more.' Rick looked into his sister's searching eyes. 'Don't worry, Georgie. Truly, there's nothing to worry about. It was a mistake—a crush I should have had on an older woman a long time ago. Jilly, you and the children are all I've got. I'm not going to do anything, ever again, to make you unhappy.'

'I'll drink to that!' Georgina turned and picked up her lime and soda. 'I think I'll have an early night if we're going sightseeing tomorrow.'

'You won't want the kids,' said Rick. 'I'll take care of them. You've earned some time on your own.'

'The kids are no trouble,' Georgina bent to kiss him. 'Maybe Missy. She tires in the heat.'

'We'll see.' He patted her hand. 'I wouldn't advise you to try climbing the Rock. Even our adventurous Prince thought better of it.'

'Quinn's climbed it,' Georgina yawned.

'He would. Halfway up and I went limp. It's well over a thousand feet and very smooth and steep.'

'But the view from the top must be fantastic!'

'How do *I* know! Ask Quinn.' Rick said his employer's name with a peculiar inflection in his voice.

'And what's that supposed to mean?' Georgina felt a rush of colour to her skin.

'I saw him look at you this morning and I was startled at what I saw,' her brother explained dryly.

'Oh?' Georgina swung back at the door, her bright, luxuriant hair framing her flushed, oval face.

'It was only there for a minute, then it vanished. He

was suddenly *the* Quinn Shieffield again—Outback Royalty, not giving a thing away. No wonder you're blushing, Georgie, I'd say he was very interested in you. Or how else do you account for that flash in his eyes? Is she happy? Is she being looked after? If you ask me, he wanted you right under his wing.'

'Well, we're only half a mile away.'

'Don't let him break your heart, Georgie,' Rick begged. 'A man like that might find it so easy—the big cattle baron with his classy accent. None of that ordinary Ocker. We just aren't part of his life. It's going to be one of those rich, snobby women who makes it to the old historic home. He's certainly knows a lot. And he's got one beautiful sister-in-law who's very fond of him.'

'There is such a thing as unholy love,' Georgina said a little tartly. 'Don't worry, Rick. I can see it as clearly as you can. I'm attracted to him, of course, I was right from the beginning, but I'm intelligent enough to doubt his serious interest in me.'

'In my opinion he'd be crazy to let you get away,' Rick said rather fiercely, his eyes on her vivid, innocent, lovely face. 'You're everything a man likes in a woman. You're lovely, sweetly sexy, you have a great figure, you love kids and dogs and animals and being outdoors. You're kind and generous and funny.'

'Were you thinking of putting me up for an award?' she looked at him with a laughing, deeply touched expression.

'You know you deserve one,' he said somewhat gruffly. 'I'd have been lost without you, Georgie—I'm that kind of person. But I don't know—this life out here, I feel kind of stronger. I wrote that letter begging Jill to come back. If I can get the boss to give me the time off, I think I'll go and get her.'

'Good idea!' Georgina clapped her hands together. 'Only, *please*, give it a little bit longer before you have another baby. Adorable as they are, I think you and Jilly have to work out a few things for yourselves.'

'What about a dog?' Rick called after her.

'Yes, you can have another dog.'

'What kind?'

'Something smaller than Tiger!'

It was to be a day Georgina would remember for ever.
Quinn came down to the bungalow soon after breakfast
and Georgina found herself taking a ride with him in a
helicopter towards the distant Olgas, the most fascinating
jumble of great domed boulders one could ever see. The
first white man to see them, more than a hundred years
before, was the explorer Ernest Giles, and he wrote:

'The appearance of Mount Olga ... is truly
wonderful. It displayed to our astonished eyes rounded
minarets, giant cupolas and monstrous domes. There
they have stood as huge memorials from the ancient
times of earth, for ages, countless eons of ages since
creation first had birth. Time, the old, the dim
magician, has ineffectually laboured here. Though all
the powers of oceans were at his command, Mount
Olga remained as it was born.'

Looking down on them from the air, as looking back
at the distant Rock, was quite unique. In the middle of
this limitless, flat isolation these phenomenal formations. It was quite easy to count the Olgas' twenty-
eight separate domes. After the recent heavy rains the
great clefts held crystal-clear pools and a wide variety of
wildflowers had sprung up like magic right across the
surrounding plains.

'The domes on the western face have been scaled,'
Quinn told her. 'They're about the same height but a
much tougher climb than the Rock.'

'Have you scaled them?' Georgina looked down in
fascination.

'Many of them,' he said. 'David and I and a few
friends of ours were forever going after adventures.'

It was the first time he had ever mentioned his
brother, Georgina reflected, and it had come out quite
naturally. 'Are we going to go down?' she asked.

'Assuredly, but first we'll drift around a little. That's King's Canyon down there. It's only recently been opened to visitors.'

'It looks lush!' Georgina exclaimed in surprise. At the head of a gorge of immense size was an oasis, with deep rock pools and a fabulous display of cycads, the tallest of which were estimated to be at least five thousand years old.

'Palm Valley,' Quinn called. 'It's the loveliest valley in the Centre. You can see all the rock pools are filled.'

'Such extraordinary cliffs!'

'Aren't they? The valley used to be part of the vast territory of the Arandas. They call the palms princes. They live together in complete isolation, enjoying their own exclusivity.'

'This has been a tremendous experience for me,' Georgina told him. 'It was an unfulfilled dream of mine to see the Centre of the continent. The *real* Australia, if you like—it's extraordinary monuments, the desert come to life. It's truly majestic. I even feel lucky enough to find Lasseter's Lost Reef.'

'The fabled "Mountain of Gold"? If it ever existed, as he said, it's still out there in the desert waiting for someone to stumble on it and make a fortune.'

'Do you think it's there?' she asked him.

'Probably.' He looked across and smiled. 'Goldmining was one of our most important industries in the early days, even though it's taken a back seat to coal, bauxite, lead, zinc, copper, iron ore, silver—you name it. Our future as a major mining nation is assured. We've made a big diamond strike and another goldfield has opened right in this State. They tell me I'm sitting on oil, so old Lasseter could very well have been telling the truth. Maybe it's somewhere in the Petermann Ranges, where he was last seen alive. It's a big country to go searching.'

'*Too* big!' said Georgina, still trying to grapple with its immensity.

'If you want to know how big,' Quinn said

humorously, 'try going across the Nullabor Plain in a bus!'

They put down in wild bush country beside what was now a magnificent billabong. At a range of perhaps two hundred feet away two red kangaroos were enjoying a playful grapple, then as the noise of the rotor settled more kangaroos hopped out of the timber belt, standing and staring at them curiously. Not so the galahs, which streaked into the sky forming a cloud of pearl grey and rose. The air pulsated with their disturbed sounds and rapid wing-beat.

Georgina turned to Quinn with pleasure. 'Aren't they beautiful?'

'You'll see many more before the day is out. If you just turn your head carefully towards me there's a magnificent sulphur-crested cockatoo, second branch up, in the ghost gum. In another second he'll take off like a supersonic jet.'

Too late.

As Georgina turned around the cockatoo flew directly away from them, shrieking mightily. A pity, because although she had seen white waves of them in the sky or dotted all over a distant tree, she had never seen one close up.

'Watch where you put your feet,' Quinn told her with a wry smile.

'What now?' Her eyes flashed all over the profusion to spinifex grass and the brilliantly red flowers of Sturt's desert pea.

'Snakes—always snakes, my girl. You're wearing boots, but it also helps to look around. A snake won't attack you unless you actually stand on it.'

'Oh, good!' All this wild beauty took on another dimension. 'Let's get further down to the water, it's so clean and shining.'

'We should have come here late evening when all the animals come down for a drink, but there's an emu right behind you.'

Georgina jerked around, but saw nothing.

'You're not accustomed to the landscape, are you?' commented Quinn.

'All the animals seem to merge with the wild. Oh, I see it. He looks charming.'

'Only the ostrich is taller,' Quinn told her.

'Oh, goodness, there's two little chicks!' she exclaimed.

'Don't sing out,' he checked her. 'The little fellows lose their stripes as they grow older. Mama there can keep pace with a jeep. I had a pet emu when I was a kid. I had a pet everything except a crocodile,' he added, 'and I guess I would have had one of them if I lived in the Top End.'

'I don't think crocodiles would be among my favourite people,' Georgina shuddered.

'I'll guarantee with the rains a few of them will come out of the tidal creeks and start wandering around places like Cairns.'

'Surely not?' Georgina had visited the tropical North Queensland city with its magnificent natural harbour, palm-studded broad streets and pleasant, prosperous buildings.

'Surely, yes.' Quinn corrected her. 'Crocodiles like to go walkabout as much as the rest of us. If you want to bet me, and I'm serious, you're on.'

Finally, at Quinn's insistence, they had to move on. 'This is going to be a big day, Georgina. I'm eager to get home. With the rains coming anything might happen. Every water-bearing stream and gully will overflow, and stock will have to be shifted. I'll pick out a spot for lunch and leave the Rock until late afternoon. The colour displays are the reason I'm leaving it until then. Every time I see them I feel totally insignificant.'

'You?' She ran back to him and smiled challengingly.

'Don't be too cheeky, we're quite, quite alone.'

'We are indeed.' She couldn't tear her eyes from his face.

'Or would you rather skip the tour and make love?'

'Didn't you just say there were snakes?' she reminded him.

'Ah, you think we'd be lying on the ground?' He grasped her arm and hurried her along. 'I think a king-sized bed would be the best situation for you and me.'

'You'll have to marry me first,' she said.

'Let's talk it out.'

'No jokes, Mr Shieffield,' she said sternly. 'You see, I believe in true love. Pure love.'

'And no dangerous adventures?' He spun her around and caught her by the shoulders.

'None lasting longer than thirty seconds.'

'Well, let's hurry.'

'Quinn!' she protested.

'Go!' He pulled her towards him and kissed her mouth, and just as she was coming dazzlingly alive he drew back abruptly and checked his watch. 'Would you please go to the helicopter, Miss Hamilton.'

'You're crazy!' She felt too excited to move.

'Go along, there's a good girl. I don't want to be forced headlong into marriage.'

The whole day Georgina was to look back on with amazement. Quinn wasn't one or two but a half a dozen people—teasing, tormenting, solicitous, instructive. He indulged her in lots of things and prevented her from doing others. His tones had all different textures, fatherly, brotherly, acidly sarcastic, and when she had supposed he was taking no notice of her at all, he would look at her plainly, as a lover. It was unbearable. She wanted to run straight into his arms, not clamber around rocks like a crazed antelope. Of course, he deliberately left those moments until a busload of tourists arrived. She hardly understood anything about him except that she was madly in love.

From the ground Ayers Rock was truly awesome, a single enormous boulder three and a half kilometres long, one and a half kilometres wide and rising three hundred and forty four metres above the vast surrounding plain. Oolera, the Sacred Dreaming Place, now changing colour before Georgina's fascinated eyes. She had seen it golden at midday against a brilliant enamel-blue sky, blood red like the plains, now through the fiery spectrum to the delicate mauves and into purple. It was the most incredible display, making it perfectly possible to understand why the aboriginals worshipped it. In the Sound Shell, a hollowed cavity shaped in a shell's flowing lines, the breeze made the weirdest sighing sounds like the sounds of a hundred mingled voices. Soft, melodic voices of the Spirits that made the aborigines move well away from the Rock and into the mulga after nightfall.

From a little distance the miraculously changing surface appeared as smooth as glass and the rare thunderstorms had transferred the great desert around it into an endless sea of silvery spinifex grass laced with everlasting daisies. For six hundred million years this Rock had been glowing.

'Incredible!' Georgina breathed quietly. The Rock that had begun as a flaming orange had now darkened to a rich purple.

'Don't turn away.' Quinn held her shoulders.

He knew what she did not. In one last mighty flare the Rock brightened, held its fire, then as though tiring of its awed human audience, lapsed back into amethyst against a luminous pale mauve sky.

After a day of almost non-stop conversation, eager questions, and verbal tussles, Georgina was very quiet on the way back to Marawalla.

'Tired?' Quinn looked at her dreamy, entranced face.

'Oh, beautifully!' Her voice was pitched sweet and low.

'I feel like picking you up and putting you to sleep on my knee.'

'Strictly speaking, you have been rather fatherly today,' she admitted.

'No doubt putting a brake on myself. I know what *I* want, but you've assured me you want marriage.'

'I'm sorry, too,' she said. 'Anyway, I love you for

taking me. You've given me a truly beautiful day, one I'll remember long after I've forgotten everything else.' And now, incredibly, her eyes were glistening with the quick tears of heightened emotion. She turned her face away from him and her small teeth clamped down on her bottom lip.

'I want you so much,' he said harshly, 'I think you'd better go home.'

Keith Bracknell insisted that Georgina stay and have a sundowner before she went back to the bungalow. She had been invited to dinner as well, but she pleaded smilingly that she was a little tired after all her exertions.

'I'll drive you back to the bungalow,' Quinn offered afterwards, and got up.

'Oh, no, not at all. Keith wants your company, and it's only a short walk.'

He still kept moving, but she put up a staying hand. 'Really, I'd like to. I love the evening air.'

'I can't help feeling she means it, Quinn,' Keith Bracknell laughed. 'I hope we see you again, Georgina. I've wanted so much to talk to you, but we've had so little time.'

'It's been marvellous!' Georgina assured him, while the two men followed her out on to the wide verandah.

'Yell when you get home,' Quinn said pleasantly.

'How about if I whistle? I have an excellent whistle.'

'That will do.' He said it as though she were about to walk alone, after dark, in New York's Central Park.

He really was the master of the about-face, Georgina thought. If he wasn't giving her the big come-on he was deciding on sending her away!

She reached the bungalow in record time, her thoughts as fevered as her feet. There were lights shimmering through the windows, and as she looked towards the side window of the small living-dining room her topaz glance became transfixed.

'Oh, my God!' She blurted the words aloud, her mind

struggling against what her eyes had seen. Rick had given her his solemn promise. He had begged Jilly to come home.

Inside the house, behind the misty curtains Rick was standing like a robot or something not quite human. His hands were up, jerking at the pale woman's hands that were locked about his neck. His rage and deep involvement were without question.

Lucinda seemed to be smiling; her strange, delicate sneer. She looked like a doll, a mannequin, before Rick's tall, boyishly lean frame. Her perfect face was dead white. Her long jet-black hair had fallen out of its flawless chignon.

'You bitch!' Georgina muttered, and seconds later was running towards the house. She felt like slapping Rick until his teeth rattled and, better yet, booting Lucinda down the stairs. She had set after Richard—no doubt about it. This wasn't some helpless passion that had invaded her body. She didn't care for him. That wasn't her way. Her way was the game of challenge—to devour the males that were attracted to her like the Black Widow spider.

And there was no excuse for Rick at all. He had a wife, a good girl he didn't deserve. A girl who was probably starving herself right now to turn herself back into the svelte Jilly he remembered. Where were the children while all this was happening?

Georgina flew up the stairs, the very picture of sisterly outrage.

'S'truth, Georgie, you're home!' Rick exclaimed almost eagerly.

'And not a minute too soon!' The glint in her eyes was thrilling. 'Where are the children?'

'They've had their bath and their tea and I've put them to bed.'

'At this hour?'

'We've been out all day,' Rick told her. 'Listen, Georgie, this isn't what you think.'

Lucinda's trill of laughter dismissed that for ever.

'No wonder your dear sister is a little shaken! Self-righteous as well. How boring!'

'And you look like a stupid doll,' Georgina said violently. 'Can't you see how wrong this is?'

'Now just a minute, Georgie,' Rick began roughly.

'You be quiet!'

'Damn women! Damn them all,' Rick grumbled.

Lucinda's brilliant black eyes were as blank and impenetrable as coal. 'You just can't order a man around like that, my dear,' she drawled. 'I guess in a year or two you'll be a real shrew.'

'I'm a real shrew now,' Georgina declared fierily. 'So beware! You've come here deliberately to cause trouble. You can't allow us to sort things out for ourselves. You're a destroyer.'

'How melodramatic!' Lucinda turned away and began doing up her hair. 'Your brother, my dear, is no good. In fact I would say he's very weak.'

'He's very young,' Georgina flashed with a bitter laugh. 'Whereas you've been doing all this grotesque fascinating for the last twenty years!'

'*Twenty* years!' Lucinda broke off what she was doing and stared at Georgina blankly. 'My dear, you're hysterical! I'm only a year or two older than you.'

'You're nearly ten years older than I am,' Georgina returned curtly, adding an extra two for good measure. 'And to make matters worse, you're just having us all on. Poor stupid Rick here can't see you for what you are.'

'Bunkum!' Rick exclaimed hotly. 'How was I to know she would come here?'

'And I gather you didn't want to kiss her either?' Georgina hurled at him scornfully.

'Oh, I don't know, Georgie,' Rick said halfheartedly, 'I did and I didn't. It's only you women who make such a big deal about kissing. As far as I'm concerned Mrs Shieffield never could and never will make any difference to my relationship with Jilly. Jilly is my *wife*.'

'You mean men are allowed their little outlets?' Georgina cried angrily.

'I mean men know what's real and what is not.'

'Hell!' groaned Georgina, trapped by the basic difference between the sexes. 'Are you paying attention to this, Mrs Shieffield?' she cried. 'Terrible as it is, I'm identifying with you for a minute. Men make a travesty of our feelings for them.'

'I already know that,' Lucinda said bitterly. 'I suspect, my dear Miss Hamilton, that you're in love with my brother-in-law. That's why you're so suffused with anger. You know very well Quinn is no more in love with you than your lightweight brother here is in love with me. They only see us in terms of our sexuality, blinding for the moment. Their real goals are sometimes quite different.'

'And so they should be,' said Rick.

'Oh, shut up, Rick,' Georgina said emotionally. 'Love is the centre of a woman's world. Above everything else her life has to do with the people she loves—husbands, children, family. Have you any idea how much time I've spent on *you*?'

'And I appreciate it, Georgie,' Rick stared at his sister with something like misery. 'God, don't I tell everyone you're the best sister in the world?'

'I really think I should be taking myself off,' Lucinda drawled. 'You're both so green you make me wince!'

'You asked for this, Mrs Shieffield,' Georgina said decisively. 'I dislike being cruel, but you were a novelty in my brother's life. You're a very beautiful woman, but quite without understanding. It's not enough to stimulate a man's fancies. They're just as happy to go back to the woman who bolsters and supports them. Rick will go back to my sister-in-law because he really fears to be without her. A lot of times, for a woman, having a husband is like having another baby.'

'Turn it off, Georgie!' snapped Rick with aggression. 'I never really know what you're talking about anyway. Lucinda—Mrs Shieffield came here without invitation.

If you like, it was a set-up. I can't deny her effect on me, but I have more important things on my mind.' His slanting golden eyes actually had a look of outrage and innocence.

'The humiliation of it!' Lucinda said, almost humorously. 'It seems to me your brother is a very large child.'

'And I can actually feel pleased about it,' Georgina said. 'It's difficult to sustain passion when the comic element creeps in. This is farce, not fascination. And now it's over.'

'Ah, yes, but still, we two remain in conflict.' Lucinda smoothed her gleaming hair and walked casually to the door. 'Some people aren't made for drama—I do see that.' She looked over her shoulder at Rick. 'But others can't escape it. You. Me. Quinn. You might be your brother's guardian angel, but there's no angel looking after you. Get in my way and you're dead!'

'Phew!' breathed Rick after she had gone.

'What a fool you are, Rick,' Georgina said sadly. She sat down abruptly in a chair and her eyes filled up with tears.

'Oh, don't cry, Georgie darling!' Rick fell on his knees beside her and took her hand. 'Let me tell you how it happened.'

'You didn't *have* to kiss her, Rick,' Georgina said bitterly.

'It's funny how different kisses can be,' Rick mused. 'It was a sort of poisoned kiss. It all happened in a dream. Really, I think she's a sort of witch. Anyway, I found I could help myself after a minute. There was Jilly behind my closed eyes. I suppose I saw what a rotten thing I was doing and then I didn't want to do it any more. I could have handled it all without you. I could have handled it alone. You want me to act like a man, but you won't let me.'

'From now on,' Georgina said tersely, 'I will. I have to go to bed, Rick—I'm exhausted.'

'But I've got your dinner hot in the oven.'

'What is it?' Georgina asked in a slightly less lifeless tone.

'You used to call it a casserole, as far as I can remember. They sent it over from the house, with some rice dish and a terrific apple pie. At least try to have some. Can't I make you understand, Georgie, you don't have to worry about me any longer. So Lucinda laid a trap for me—us, what does it matter? To tell you the truth, I think she was half tipsy. All this *femme fatale* stuff can get very boring.'

Georgina made a sound that was as much a cry of pain as a laugh. 'No wonder women question man's capacity for long-term fidelity! They've only got about one-third of a woman's staying power, devotion, fidelity, call it what you will.'

'I don't know why you'd say that, Georgie,' Rick said piously. 'All in all, Jilly and I have a happy marriage.'

'Tell that to Jilly,' Georgina said harshly, 'and I just hope she pays attention.'

'Don't be too hard on me, Georgie,' Rick begged. 'I haven't really done anything, you know. This kind of thing must happen to a lot of people. It's not difficult to be attracted to someone other than the one you love. I should think it would be a terrible period if both parties cared, but Lucinda doesn't care about me. Which makes her actions, to say the least, weird. All the feeling she's got is directed towards Quinn. It's the kind of thing I can't understand—all this intense hate and love and anger. She's right about one thing, I'm not the type for turmoil, I want to live in peace with my wife and children. I want my only sister to be proud of me.'

Georgina shook her head as if to clear it. 'The fact is, you haven't really done anything,' she said.

'What's a couple of kisses?' Rick threw in breezily.

'Enough to nearly lose you your wife,' she reminded him sharply. 'What the heck have we both got into, coming here to Rambulara? Their ways aren't ours. There are some experiences, I suppose, we can do without.'

'Such as?'

They were viewing one another so tenderly, protectively, neither of them heard Quinn's cat-treaded approach. Now Georgina sprang up and looked towards the door. 'Quinn! You startled me!' she exlcaimed.

'You're making that very clear.' He moved into the bungalow and nodded to Rick. 'My sister-in-law just went past me. She's been here?'

'Yes, sir,' Rick answered unflinchingly.

'I wonder if she was invited?'

'Hardly, sir,' Rick protested. 'I'm quite aware of my place in the scheme of things.'

'Georgina?' Quinn gave her a swift, piercing look that noted and wanted to account for the abnormal brightness of her eyes and the hectic flush in her cheeks.

'I was speaking to Mrs Shieffield for a while. She wanted to know about our trip.'

Rick nodded his head as if agreeing readily. 'I wonder if I could ask you something, sir,' he said manfully. 'I'd very much like to bring my wife home.'

'I should damned well think so!' Quinn responded abruptly, still looking at Georgina. 'I don't exactly go along with these separate holidays.'

'You know the reason, sir,' Rick said quietly. 'We had a few difficult moments, but you can be sure they're over. With your permission I'd like to go for Jill as soon as possible.'

'I never approved of her leaving in the first place,' Quinn told him. 'In fact, I would have gone after her right there and then.'

'I expect so,' said Rick, with downcast eyes.

There was silence for a moment and Georgina filled it. 'She needed a little time on her own,' she pointed out encouragingly. 'Young mothers sometimes have a little depressive attack.'

'Especially when they think they're not loved,' Quinn said curtly. 'All right, Rick. We're going to be hellishly busy, but I'm giving you a week off. You don't have to bring your wife back immediately. Have a few days together. Make it a second honeymoon.'

'That sounded like an order,' Rick grinned.

'It was.' Quinn wasn't going to smile at him. 'There's no sense in coming back with us in the morning. You can arrange your flight from here. Well, what *is* it?'

Rick was obviously troubled about something. 'I haven't much money, sir. I didn't think I'd be needing it.'

'I can get you some,' Georgina said quickly, looking embarrassed.

'Will you kindly let your brother work on being an independent person,' Quinn said gently. 'I'll give you an advance on your wages,' he told Rick crisply. 'I'm also raising them, as you're starting to fit in. I've had good reports of you from my brother-in-law. If you can tone down the excess exuberance you'll be given progressively more responsible work. It's obvious you love the life— and I would have thought Jill did too?'

'Oh, she does, sir!' A dozen emotions were crossing Rick's expressive face—astonishment, pleasure, a quick eagerness. 'I promise you I'll do everything I can to make it all happen. Even since I've been a child I've longed for this space and freedom. I was born for the Outback life.'

'What about you, Georgina?' Quinn looked at her more or less mockingly.

'It's almost time for me to go home,' she pointed out quietly. 'My boss didn't put an exact date on my return, but as soon as Rick and Jill return, I must go.'

'I wish you didn't have to.' Some of the bright pleasure in Rick's eyes began to fade. 'I know it's not exactly usual to be so attached to one's sister, but Georgie and I have had a funny life. We share a deep devotion. It's as simple as that.'

'And I quite understand, believe me,' Quinn answered, unexpectedly. 'Georgina does her damnedest to keep up with everything that's asked of her, but her strength mightn't be always equal to the task. *You* have to be able to function on your own, as a man should. It's the man who should carry much of the burden. I want all this reliance on your sister to stop here. She has a lot of living to do for herself.'

'Yes, sir.' Rick straightened his wide shoulders. 'This afternoon I kissed goodbye to my boyhood.'

'That was pretty idiotic, wasn't it?' Quinn returned dryly.

'You know what I mean, sir.'

'I suppose I do.' Quinn glanced towards Georgina, slumped rather dejectedly in an armchair. 'You look as if you need an early night.'

'What time do we leave in the morning?' She lifted her curly head.

'We're cleared for take-off at seven sharp. I'll have your advance for you then, Rick—in cash, so you won't have any problems. You have just one week and I'll expect to see you back with the wife I first met.' Quinn turned and walked towards the door, and for all her tiredness and strange depression Georgina followed him.

'Thank you for what you're doing for Rick,' she spoke softly into the cool, evening air.

'I wonder if I'd have been quite so understanding without you.' He took her hand and drew her away from the stairs. 'What was Lucinda up to? Her tricks?'

Georgina shook her head. 'I really don't know. They were just talking.'

'So you don't propose to tell me?'

'Nothing to tell,' she shrugged.

'That had better be the truth,' said Quinn hardly.

'Why, are you jealous?' she said wildly. It just happened.

'Don't be so bloody stupid,' he retorted with more than a touch of hauteur. 'Occasionally you need someone to put you across their knee.'

'You've spoken before about wanting to slap me.' A turbulence of emotions were bringing her to the boil.

'I'm sorry, darling,' he said cuttingly, 'I only want to break your heart.'

'Well, let me tell you,' she retorted flamingly, 'you don't have that power.'

'No?' Effortlessly he twisted her and removed her from the light. 'I've learned a lot about you, Georgina. In fact I know more about you than your own brother. You're pretending now, all this fire. What you're really suffering from is a depletion of the spirit. You don't want to go home, do you? You want to stay here with me. Not for a few weeks or a few months or even years. You want to stay with me for ever.'

She answered without hesitation. 'I do *not!*' If she admitted it she would be surrendering her will for ever. Bowing down to his superior force.

'All right,' said Quinn in a brittle voice, 'it's going to take a little longer. In some ways your taking over as head of your own family hasn't been good. It means you want to fight me just for the hell of it. Really, Georgina, you don't like anyone else to have the authority.'

'You are hurting me,' she said very carefully, spacing the words.

'Call Rick,' he jeered.

She was quivering with a mixture of emotions more powerful than anger. He was holding her wrists, really not hurting her at all. She wanted to slump forward and rest her aching head against his chest. She was certain he was a man to lean on.

'Are you going to sleep?' he asked.

'I couldn't—I feel so violent.'

'That's all the pretending you're doing. You're a complex creature, Georgina. You like to provoke and then withdraw. You've been trying to hold on to your safe little life, but it just fell away when we met.'

'I know,' Georgina whispered vehemently, 'and it scares me. 'You're the best and the worst man I've ever met. If I let you . . . if I let you . . .'

He curled his hand around her chin, a gesture so possessive yet so tender she started to shake. 'You've got so much love to give, Georgina, yet you're frightened of being taken.'

'I'm so tired,' she said faintly, 'I'm going to cry.'

'That doesn't sound like you,' he mocked her gently. 'My brave, spunky Georgina!'

'I am not brave about you.'

'Love with you is a once-in-a-lifetime-thing, isn't it?' She shook her head unhappily. 'When I give my love I don't think I could ever take it back.'

'And you doubt a man could feel the same. How you are strange!'

'But we scarcely know one another, Quinn.' She looked up at him, seemingly unaware he was holding her tightly.

'The fact is I feel I've known you all my life. That years have passed instead of weeks. I'm not just talking about the immediate physical response, but all kinds of communication. You're my kind of woman, Georgina. *My* woman. My task is to get you to believe it.'

'Does that include making love to me?' she asked feverishly. 'What if you decided I didn't satisfy your desire?'

'If you're not damned careful,' he said shortly, 'you'll find out.'

'Aunty!' a little voice whispered.

'Dear God!' Quinn murmured almost inaudibly. 'I knew you'd wake someone.'

'What is it, darling?' Georgina broke away and hurried over to the open window. 'Can't you sleep?'

'I heard your voice. You woke me up.' Timmy settled his elbows on the sill. 'Hello, Mr Shieffield. Did you have a nice day?'

'Perfect, Timmy!' Quinn laughed with a burst of good humour. 'And how was your day?'

'Marvellous! Couldn't have been better. Missy went to sleep, of course.'

'Well, I think you'd better too, again.'

'I just wanted to be sure it was Aunty. She sounds like Mummy sometimes.'

'And Mummy is coming home next week,' Georgina promised him.

'Well we all want her to,' Timmy said steadily, waved to them, then turned away to climb back into bed.

'I'll go,' said Quinn. 'Take my advice and get a good night's sleep.'

'Will you pick us up in the morning?'

'Yes.' His hand came out and gently caressed her cheek. A single gesture, yet it nearly had her crying aloud with frustration. 'The next time you attempt to ignite my ignoble passions, I'm going to make darn sure we're alone.'

'Brute force doesn't count,' she said perversely, unable to resist turning her cheek into his palm.

'Fierce words from a kitten. Goodnight, Georgina. Sleep well.'

They thought they were alone, unnoticed in the vast darkness, but lost within a grove of trees, less than thirty feet from them, a woman in a green dress stood watching them with tears streaming out from the corners of her eyes.

'You'll pay,' she wailed silently. 'I *saw* you. Damn you. *Damn you! Damn you both to hell!*'

Hatred and jealousy flailed at her, disturbing the balance of her mind and leaving open a forbidden door. Branches surrounded her like a cave and she stood breathless, engulfed by violence as the one man she had ever loved walked past her, deep in thought.

She wanted to run straight at him, screaming. She wanted something in her hand so she could kill him. Instead she moved very quietly and made her way secretly around the side of the homestead. No one was about, and she went quickly down the corridor and into a bedroom, where she collapsed over the bed. She was having trouble getting her breath, the tears that were heaving in her burning like acid.

She had to get rid of Georgina Hamilton. Something small. Something easy. Like an accident.

CHAPTER TEN

DESPITE the March rains the drought still could not be considered broken. With so much at stake no one could bear to consider false alarms; they had happened before. Considerable atmospheric moisture had built up over the drought-stricken Inland several times before during the course of the summer. There was no real reason why there should be a terrible reversal, but until a more normal pattern had been established no one dared build their hopes too high. The gods were fickle—even Billy's rain gods.

Yet even when they returned to Rambulara the results of the recent storms were spectacular. The pink parakeelya extended for miles. The thick fleshy leaves of this colourful succulent could keep bullocks alive through many weeks without a drop of water. Given only a shower this arid desert region could paradoxically turn into a garden. The red earth was carpeted with wild orange, the white, gold, pink and purple of the transient wildflowers. A desert that wasn't really a desert at all.

The children thought it was fairyland, delighting in the brilliant variety of flowers, the great colonies of birds that rejoiced in the return of the water. Georgina had never seen anything to equal the great flights of budgerigars unfurling green fire across the skies. It seemed incredible, when so many people kept one or two in a cage. There had to be thousands, thousands, thousands of twittering gems of all kinds. She felt desolated that she would have to leave it. For all the profundity of her emotions, the terrible affinity she had with Quinn Shieffield, it was as though something was warning her that it was not meant to be. She felt a powerful offensive force directed at her. In her beautiful topaz eyes was a look of fear that had never been there before. Loving Quinn Shieffield was mad and hopeless and crazy. It seemed incredible that she had allowed things to get this far. Or had she *allowed* anything? She had only looked up into his eyes.

'Could we please have a swim in Mr Shieffield's pool this afternoon, Aunty?' asked Timmy. 'I want to show Mummy I can nearly swim the length.'

'Darling, I don't really know.' Georgina felt the sudden thump in her chest. She had taken little advantage of Quinn's kind offer for the simple reason that she dreaded running into Lucinda.

'Oh, *please*—Mr Shieffield said you should!' Timmy begged.

'When did he say that?' Georgina asked in surprise.

'Yesterday, when he rode up. He said he wanted us to use it. That was what it was for.'

'*Please*, Aunty!' Melissa came to cling to her.

'Oh, all right, but let me make this perfectly clear. You must do exactly as you're told, and if we see Mrs Shieffield—Timmy, this is for *you*—we must be polite.'

'Oh, great!' Timmy cried jubilantly. 'Anyway, I'll take my water pistol and if she says anything I'll zap her.'

'*Timmy!*' Georgina clutched at his arm, but Timmy ran away, excitedly calling for Tiger to come out and play ball.

'Sweet, adorable little darlings!' Aunt Edwina exclaimed, as she looked down at the children's flushed, excited faces.

'Quinn said we might use the pool,' Georgina explained.

'Of course, of course!' Aunt Edwina enthused. 'As soon as I take my pill I'm going to come out and join you.' She put out a hand and caressed Melissa's fluffy curls. 'Then when it's all finished we'll have afternoon tea.'

'What the devil are they doing here?' Lucinda demanded of Aunt Edwina as she crossed back through the entrance hall.

'Well, I never, Lucinda!' Aunt Edwina exclaimed. 'You sometimes speak to me as though I'm a servant in my own house!'

'*My* house, too, Aunt Edwina,' Lucinda said almost warningly.

'I don't think so, my dear. I know you've been telling me for a long time, but the truth of it is quite different. We've all tried to be kind to you, but it has never been easy. You're determined on something you can never achieve. You were *David's* wife, Lucinda, that's all. Poor, poor David who adored you. You weren't content to make him miserable, you destroyed him.'

Lucinda's finely chiselled lips jerked nervously back from her teeth. 'My God, what are you saying?'

Aunt Edwina, who had begun strongly, even sternly, now became uncertain and vague. 'I promised I'd put on a good afternoon tea for the children. Excuse me, Lucinda. There just isn't anyone who can help you.'

Palms encircled the cool oasis of the pool area, the blue intensity of the sky reflected in the brilliant water.

'Oh, we're going to have fun!' exclaimed Aunt Edwina.

'I can't swim,' Melissa said forlornly.

'I'll show you, Missy,' her brother said. 'But really I want to have a swim on my own first.'

'Very well, in you go.' Georgina stood with her little niece beneath the huge sunflower umbrella winding her hair into a knot on top of her head. 'We'll have a nice little paddle on the step. You're going to keep your hat on, Missy, I don't want you to burn.' Her hair out of the way, she bent down and kissed Melissa on the cheek. 'Oh, you smell good! Is that my perfume?'

'Yes, Aunty.'

'I'll be sure to pick another hiding place.' Hand in hand they wandered over to the pool, Georgina in a very stylish bronze maillot that displayed her beautiful figure and Melissa in a blue and white frilly two-piece with a matching mob-cap that came down over her eyes.

And there Aunt Edwina found them about ten minutes later. 'Let me look after Melissa while you have a swim,' she suggested kindly, and gave the little girl a glance of tender affection.

'We'll sit under the brolly,' Melissa smiled.

'And I've arranged for us to have afternoon tea here.' Aunt Edwina pressed the little hand that slipped into hers. 'Let's sit down and watch how Aunty swims.'

Lucinda, too, watched from an upstairs window. She never knew exactly where she was with the old lady. Mad as a hatter, of course, yet she could say the most appallingly perceptive things.

For Georgina it was good to put all her nagging anxieties aside. She loved the water, cutting through it with the ease and speed of an excellent swimmer, making circles around Timmy, who squealed with delight, diving to show him how easy it was when done correctly.

'I shall miss you terribly when you go,' Aunt Edwina told her later as the children were playing. 'You seem to have become so familiar in such a short time. I have difficulty remembering I haven't always known you.'

'I know I won't forget you, Aunt Edwina,' Georgina replied quietly. 'Do you ever visit Quinn's sister in the Territory?'

'Oh, much, much too hot for me!' the old lady exclaimed. 'A different kind of heat—not dry, but humid. I couldn't take it any more, but you young people seem to thrive on it, just like the plants. Old ladies aren't cut out for the jungle.'

'I would have liked to have met Quinn's sisters,' Georgina said reflectively. 'Are they like him?'

'All of the children are good-looking,' Aunt Edwina said, and her mouth trembled. 'Anne is the most like Quinn. They both have that black hair and blue eyes—a stunning contrast. Serena is lovely too, but she's her mother's side of the family—light brown hair, green eyes. D-David was a mixture of both sides of the family. In a funny way he could look and sound like

Quinn sometimes, though their colouring was different. But they both had that good profile and cultured, resonant voices. That's why she married him, you know.'

Georgina remained silent, not knowing what to say.

'She was in his blood. He always loved her, even when they were children and both following Quinn around. Quinn was always the leader. David adored his brother. It was she who made him change.' Aunt Edwina gazed at Georgina in a dazed way, almost as though she was barely seeing her. 'She's a monster.'

'Aunt Edwina!' Georgina was so shocked she reached out and grasped the old lady's hand.

'Billy recognised that at once. Even when she was a little girl, Billy would move off as soon as he saw her. He has special powers, you know. He recognises people for what they are. He knew years ago that Lucinda would bring tragedy to this house. He calls her a special name in his dialect. I don't know what it means. She lied to him.'

'Aunt Edwina, you're upsetting yourself.' The frail, paper-dry hand in Georgina's was shaky. 'Don't let's talk any more about it. You've taken your pill and you must allow it to work.' Georgina knew by now that the old lady had a heart condition.

'But she's starting *again*!' Aunt Edwina quavered.

'Now I can't allow this,' said Georgina. 'If you're worried or frightened about something you must tell Quinn. He would never allow anything or anyone to upset you.'

'Please, Georgina,' the old lady persisted. 'I can trust you, can't I?'

'Of course you can—but you're becoming so agitated.' Georgina found herself masssaging the small, frail hand. It was difficult to communicate ease and calm when one was feeling anxious oneself. 'Is there anything in particular that's worrying you?'

'Oh, please God, no,' Aunt Edwina said shakily.

'I'm sure you have nothing to fear, Aunt Edwina.'

Georgina looked into the distressed blue eyes that still had violet lights in them. 'Is it something Mrs Shieffield said?'

'She hasn't changed a bit.'

'Please speak to Quinn,' Georgina implored.

The old lady nodded but could not speak, so Georgina moved closer and clasped her. The frail form was shaking like a small child. 'If Lucinda is upsetting you so much I think she should go away. She's still a young woman with a life of her own to lead.'

'She's a changeling,' said Aunt Edwina. 'Someone the wicked fairies left on the Halletts' doorstep. They wanted her so badly they were prepared to do anything. Now they don't want her at all. They want her to stay away—especially her mother. She blames herself, you see for her part in it all.'

'In her daughter's unhappy marriage?' Georgina faltered.

But Aunt Edwina wasn't given to answering direct questions. 'She drove David mad before the end. He suffered so much.'

'It's no good to go over it, Aunt Edwina, though I know you can't forget.'

Aunt Edwina looked drained white, really, really old. She pressed her hand into the crook of Georgina's elbow. 'She lied to him, I'm sure. I could have sworn I heard her, but my mind plays tricks on me sometimes. She said she wanted a divorce, that she and Quinn wanted to be together. She laughed that wicked laugh of hers. She made David believe Quinn had betrayed his own brother.'

'And David believed this?' Georgina asked sharply, feeling sick inside.

'They said he'd been drinking, but he was, without question, sober that day. Lucinda told me I'd dreamed it all up and I would be sent away for ever if I told such a terrible story—but I had to tell someone. Now I know better. I didn't dream it, child. I *remember*!'

Aunt Edwina began to cry and Georgina stroked her

snow-white head. 'You can't be blamed for anything,' she said intensely. 'It's in some people's nature to destroy, but I still think David had a tragic accident. He would have been frightfully upset, yes, mad and angry with his wife, but I can't believe he would accept his brother's guilt. You understand, don't you, Aunt Edwina—it was a lie?'

'Oh, yes, a wicked lie!' the old lady said firmly, throwing her head up. 'Such a thing would have been unspeakable, unthinkable to Quinn. All those years of looking after his brother! He wouldn't have hurt him for the world. Why, Lucinda and David had to run away to get married. Quinn would never have allowed it. He had come to see Lucinda for what she really was. How could he let her marry his brother?'

'I guess David was a man exercising his right to live his own life. People don't function as well as they normally do when they're in a wretched state. That seems to have been what happened. So much happening inside his head some fatal error was made. *I* know and *you* know that what Lucinda said, if she said it, was an unspeakable lie. What I don't understand is how she expected to carry it off. I can't, absolutely cannot accept that Quinn would betray his own brother. I don't even care if he did love her or she was his dark sorceress, you only have to know him.' Georgina drew a short, sharp, emotional breath. 'This is terrible, Aunt Edwina!'

'And now I've upset you,' quavered Aunt Edwina.

'It's all right. I'm just getting a bit emotional.' Georgina lifted a hand and dashed a tear away from her eyes. 'Some people must have to live with a great deal of guilt and fear. I wouldn't be Lucinda for the world.'

'You *couldn't* be,' Aunt Edwina asserted. 'Look, here are the children coming back. We'd better smile or they'll see that we're unhappy. It will be better for you, Georgina, to go back to the city until these issues are settled. Quinn has been more generous towards Lucinda than anyone could have expected. If I'd gone to him with my story I think he might have killed her. I've never forgotten his anguish the day David was carried in. When they were boys he was always looking after him, more like a father than a big brother. He has never heard a whisper of what we now believe.'

'And he must never hear it,' Georgina pleaded. 'We must spare him the pain.'

'You love him, don't you?' Aunt Edwina asked softly.

'You know I do,' Georgina said quietly.

'I wondered why you were so familiar the first time I saw you. All the time I thought I'd known you when you were growing up. I was certain I'd seen you walking through the house, yet we've never had anyone with your colouring in the family before. Such strange fancies come on me at times.'

Timmy rushed up to them and hung on Georgina's arm. 'May I go in for a swim again, please, Aunty? I'm so hot!'

'I like sitting under the brolly best,' Melissa smiled.

With a sudden spurt of energy Aunt Edwina tapped the cushioned chair beside her. 'Missy, Melissa,' she said, 'what a pretty name for a pretty girl.'

Ten minutes later Quinn walked across the terrace to join them on the lawn. 'You look very well in a swimsuit, Georgina,' he said with a mocking smile.

It was no use. She couldn't return the smile.

'You look beautiful too, Missy.'

At least Melissa loved it, her satin cheeks going rosy. 'Aunt Edwina said she had a doll she was going to give me,' she said importantly.

'I thought she might,' Quinn put out a hand and touched his great-aunt lightly. 'It's a great honour to have one from the collection.'

'You know, you've to look after it, Missy,' Aunt Edwina said calmly. 'It's to look at and love more than to play with.'

'I'll keep her on my bed,' Melissa decided.

Timmy, still in the pool, shouted and waved, and Aunt Edwina suddenly pushed herself to her feet. 'I've just remembered a letter I must write. Excuse me, children, won't you?'

'May I sit on the step and paddle, Quinn?' Melissa asked.

'I don't see why not. I'll keep an eye on you.' He patted her lightly on the head as she ran past.

'The kids seem to be enjoying themselves.' He shifted Georgina's long legs slightly and sat down on the recliner beside her. 'What's wrong with you?'

'God knows,' she said moodily, so emotionally vulnerable she wanted to cry.

'Aunt Edwina has grown very fond of you.'

'Yes.' She looked around for her cover-up but couldn't see it.

'Please don't put it on,' he said.

'What?'

'Whatever enveloping garment you're looking for. What I don't understand is, you've got all that marmalade hair and golden eyes and you haven't got one single freckle.' He glanced from her face, down her body and her long, slender legs. 'You look incredibly, perversely, innocently sexy.' He took her hand.

'Behave yourself, Mr Shieffield,' she said shakily.

'What about coming for a ride with me this afternoon? Somewhere not a soul can find us.'

'That's dumb.'

'Not dumb at all. Play your cards right and I might forget I hate the thought of marriage.'

'I'm going home soon,' she said.

'Go home. I can come after you.' His blue eyes were sparkling. 'This is hell, Georgina, not being able to touch you, and so much skin!'

'You needn't look,' she reminded him.

'What's wrong with you, really?' he asked gently. 'You look sad.'

'I am sad,' she sighed.

'Can't confront the fact that you're in love with me?'

'What about that interview?' she said.

'Don't be a pest, darling.'

'I hate it when you call me darling,' she said, and her voice shook.

'I'm sorry. I'll call you brat. It's very hot—I think you'd better get out of the sun.'

'I'll go and cool off in the water.' She swung her legs away from him and got up.

'I suppose if you weren't the way you are, you wouldn't be a woman,' Quinn said laconically. He walked around the end of the recliner and approached her, poised like a startled fawn. 'So long, brat,' he said. 'You'll come around when you're ready.'

'Why must men be so arrogant?' she sighed.

'It's the only damn way that makes sense.' He pulled her towards him and while she shook with fright bent his head and kissed her mouth. 'I wouldn't even know if I want to marry you,' he said shortly.

It was Timmy in the water who let out an enraptured whistle. He had seen so much in his short life, but he had never expected to see Mr Shieffield kiss Aunty.

Standing before the shuttered windows of her bedroom, Lucinda had a perfect view of the pool area. A perfect view of Georgina's slender body, long satiny legs pressed against Quinn. He was holding her so that her hair spilled back over her shoulder and down her back. They made a monstrously compelling picture. Another one of those pictures Lucinda could not erase from her mind. If she was going to do anything at all, best to do it while the brother was away. Quinn could never be allowed to have a life without her. He had belonged to her since childhood.

Later that afternoon when the children were resting with Lulah, Georgina took her accustomed ride.

'Keep away from the Jump-Up, won't you?' Lucinda warned her. 'They're yarding a large mob.'

'Where would you suggest?' Georgina shaded her

eyes and looked away in the direction of the shimmering plains.

'Four Mile Creek might be the best,' Lucinda said abruptly, signalling to a distant stable-boy to take care of her horse. 'The men are far too busy to keep you out of trouble.'

'Thank you. I'll be careful to keep out of the way.' Georgina turned her mare's head around and rode away. For a moment she thought she saw a swirl of dust in the far distance, but when she looked again she thought she was mistaken. That was the direction of Four Mile Creek. In any case, the red dust had been laid with the rain.

She had only a few days to go and she wanted to lock as much as she could of Rambulara away in her memory. What Aunt Edwina had told her had upset her dreadfully. Yet for all Lucinda's accusations she knew in her heart that Quinn had not been Lucinda's lover during the bitter, tragic period of her marriage to his brother. But had she ever really released him? There was something between them. She lived on Rambulara when she had the money to build her own house anywhere in the world. No one seemed to like her. Indeed, Quinn's aunt and uncle had flown off to Adelaide when they had been expected to stay on at least another week. Aunt Edwina disliked and feared Lucinda, yet still she stayed. Georgina recalled glances and gestures that seemed to fall into place. As for her, Quinn was certainly attracted to her. Perhaps he might even go so far as to consider marriage; a defensive wall to keep Lucinda out.

The mare wanted to be given its head, and Georgina answered the summons. An affection had developed between the two of them, and she turned her back on her old ride and galloped in the direction of the creek, while a flock of corellas wheeled overhead in a white gale. How she would miss all this!

A moment later she screamed aloud as a rifle shot rang out from the belt of acacias away to the west of

her. Something whistled past her ear and her skin
turned bloodless. God, someone was shooting at her! It
just wasn't possible. She was riding in the wrong place,
in a danger zone. Another shot was fired off. The
mare's smooth action had turned into terrified huge
strides. It was impossible to gather her in; impossible to
clear a fallen tree that had gone over in the fury of a
recent storm.

Georgina leaned forward to go into that ill-prepared
jump while the mare made a gallant, frenzied effort to
clear it. The next thing Georgina knew, the flower-
tangled earth was flying up to meet her. She tried to
tuck herself into a loose ball without even the time or
the breath to cry out.

She rolled. She wasn't hurt. Then as she warmed into
wild relief she slammed into a log half hidden by
Mitchell grass and was knocked unconscious.

The wind blew the sounds of the shots towards them,
but even as the men sprang towards their horses it was
too late. The cattle were already on the run. They swept
past the pens with a terrifying din, bellowing their fright
and fury, ready to run until they dropped.

Quinn caught the reins of his horse and leapt into the
saddle, cursing the fool who had fired those shots. What
the hell was he doing? He would skin the lunatic alive!

'Let's go!'

Quinn was the first to move off, with his foreman
yelling to the men behind him. Spider, the best of the
stockboys, was already moving out to the left. With any
luck they could turn the beasts before they ran their
hard-won condition off. Just ten minutes more and they
would have been yarded.

Swearing violently, Quinn pressed his horse harder
and harder, while the big black demonstrated its
magnificent qualities. If he could gain the lead bullock,
it was dangerous, but he might be able to swerve
diagonally across the face of the stampede, cut it to a
stone stop.

'Hyaaa! Hyaaa!' Stock whips unfurled, cracking out over the thunder of the galloping hooves.

Some of the weaker cattle were going down, pounded beneath the hooves of the stronger beasts. The longer the stampede lasted, the greater the losses.

'Boss!' Spider's loud voice rose yelling.

But he had seen her—a woman. No trick of the light. She had just appeared out of the grass.

Quinn felt the icy sweat break out all over his body. She wasn't moving. She was standing perfectly still, on the verge of destruction.

For the men behind him, it was scarcely less horrific. Where had she come from? What was she doing?

The big black stallion was turning on a terrific burst of speed, its flashing legs charging like pistons. Every man was riding hammeringly into the mob, cursing and praying, hearts pounding in shock. If Quinn couldn't head the mob off all the danger each one of them was inviting would be in vain. The girl would be trampled. They all recognised her now. Her hair seemed to catch fire in the golden air. She looked tiny, very much alone, standing oddly as if she had no idea of the danger she was in.

Before he could even think of his own peril Quinn drove the stallion right across the mob's path. His men behind him felt themselves freeze, realising that if this appalling piece of daring failed, not one but two people would be mercilessly trampled. And the stallion? A magnificent aniimal would be dashed to death.

It was a moment all of them would relive in nightmares; a charge that lasted moments but brought the terrified beasts to a bewildered stop. Still bellowing, they milled around together, a solid wall of quivering flesh.

Spider slipped out of his saddle and felt his legs buckle under him. He hadn't thought it possible to live through such terror and come out at the other side.

Ashen under his tan, Quinn wheeled back to where Georgina was swaying, her hand to her temple.

'What lunacy is this?' Quinn cried out to her. His mind, his whole body had suffered a severe shock. He had been prepared to give his life to save her; now he wanted to whip some sense into her.

'*Quinn.*' Her voice was only a breathless little flutter.

One look at her dazed expression, the incomprehension in her eyes, and he was out of the saddle, supporting her, his eyes coming to rest on the swelling, bruised contusion on her temple. His arm tightened around her waist and he jerked his head around looking for her horse.

'Georgina, what happened?' he demanded.

'Someone shot at me. Imagine!'

He gave her an astounded look that darkened into a terrible considering. 'Can you walk?' he asked shortly.

'I think so.' She frowned at him, his dark face going wavy.

'You don't have to, I promise you.' Supporting her, he snapped his head around as his foreman rode up. 'Go for the jeep, will you, Mick? Spider and the rest of them can yard the cattle. Stay with them until they settle.'

'Is she all right, Boss?' the foreman's normally ruddy face was pale and worried.

'Concussed, by the look of it. Doesn't seem to have broken anything. Her horse must be around some place.'

'What about those shots that were fired?' Mick demanded. 'Who the hell was responsible for that? I can't think of anyone fool enough to fire near a mob.'

'Get the jeep, please, Mick.' Quinn said bleakly. 'I'll find out who's responsible.'

'Sure, Boss.' Mick looked away from that taut, closed face.

'My head aches,' Georgina murmured, and looked at Quinn as though he could explain why.

'I'll have a doctor fly in and take a look at it.'

'Oh, yes,' she sighed.

'Don't talk, Georgina,' he said.

But she just stared at him with her great amber eyes. 'You nearly got yourself killed,' she told him in wonderment. 'You nearly got yourself killed for *me*.'

'You didn't really think you were going to get away from me?'

It was useless to say any more. For a second Georgina continued to stare at him, then she slumped sideways into his arms.

CHAPTER ELEVEN

It took Georgina a full week to recover from her concussion, and in the space of that time, Jill returned to her husband and children and Lucinda, still denying her terrible part in Georgina's accident and the subsequent stampede, was banished from Rambulara for ever.

'You feel sorry for her, yet she might have killed you?' Jill, of the two of them, seemed the more upset. 'I think it was a murderous thing to do, and she should have been punished.'

'Call the police, you mean?'

'Certainly. Put her in jail.'

'Attempted what?' queried Georgina. 'Frightening me out of my wits? She denied everything, you know—swore she was back at the house all the time. No rifle was missing and she didn't even own one.'

'She could have got one easily,' said Jilly. 'I think the whole thing's damned odd. And now Quinn took an incredible risk to save you neither of you seem to be talking.'

'What's there to talk about?' Georgina said strangely. 'I feel absolutely numb.'

'You of all people!' Jilly wailed. 'I only hope she realises how incredibly generous you were to her, not wanting an investigation.'

'I didn't want to punish her,' Georgina explained. 'I certainly couldn't punish the Shieffield family. They've had enough. Besides, life catches up with us very well. Quinn mightn't have called in the police, but he certainly called in her father. I don't think I've ever seen a man look more grim in my life.'

'She seemed afraid of him,' said Jilly.

'Perhaps enough to try and pull herself together.'

177

Georgina's amber head rested back against the planter's chair, her arms extended along its sides. She still looked rather pale and she had lost weight, so her fine bone structure was extremely pronounced.

'How are you really feeling, Georgie,' Jill asked. 'You know I love you like my own sister and I'm worried about you. So's Rick. We accept that you had an accident and a nasty shock—but there's something else, isn't there?'

'Nothing.' Georgina looked up and smiled. 'Only delayed reaction. Rick and the children are so glad to have you home again, I guess I'm a wet blanket.'

'Never!' Jilly remonstrated with her. She was sitting opposite her sister-in-law, her fair hair cut in a pert bob, her petite figure trim and neat in yellow cotton jeans and a cowl-neck navy cotton T-shirt. Her lovely skin was lightly gilded, and whatever wounds had been inflicted on her self-esteem they now seemed entirely healed. She looked, acted, sounded stronger, more mature, and the few days alone she had spent with her husband had more than reaffirmed her all-important role in his life.

It was Georgina now who seemed so very vulnerable. Georgina who appeared to be suffering some crisis.

From another room in the bungalow came a cry of pleasure as Timmy put together his handsome new present, a Lego space station. 'Being away from Rick and the children was worse than anything I've ever known,' Jilly sighed. 'It's so good, *good* to be together again.' She turned her head and gazed in an oval ornamental mirror. 'I won't let myself get out of hand again.'

'And may you never encounter anyone remotely like Lucinda Shieffield,' Georgina added fervently. 'So beautiful, and in my view unbalanced. People like that don't even seem to have a conscience. Yet I pity her. All she seems to have is the past. Last night I dreamt she'd come back.'

'Never!' Jill disagreed adamantly. 'Whatever Quinn

said to her it was absolutely final. I saw him at the time, and I can assure you his feelings would have got through even to Lucinda. Some people are better at conveying strong feeling than others, and Lucinda couldn't delude herself it was anything other than the most explosive detestation. It made my blood run cold just to see the way he looked at her. It was loathing, Georgie, disgust.'

She said it as though she desperately wanted to ease Georgina's heart, but Georgina strangely seemed quite uninterested. 'Quinn must be back,' she said quietly, 'isn't that the plane coming in?'

'Yes.' Jill walked out on to the verandah, saw Quinn's plane circle the compound and come in for a landing. 'You're being a bit hard on him lately, aren't you?'

Georgina shrugged. 'Yes, I am.' She came to stand beside Jilly and lifted her face to the warm, scented air. 'I'm glad he's home.' Thunder was rumbling, shaking the heavens with a deep-throated, dull roar, and the birds in their legions were winging for cover. Every stream and gully on the great property was running water and a miraculous change had come over the harsh world. The Inland had two faces; one of immense cruelty, the other of burning hills, sapphire skies and millions of sweet flowers that laced the red sands.

'The divine blessing,' Jill whispered, her eyes on the huge pile-up of storm clouds. 'The drought is only a terrible memory now.'

'Billy has taken credit,' Georgina smiled. 'Billy and the Royals.'

'Did you ever see anything like that?' Jilly pointed to the brilliant and quite strange atmospheric effects. Haloes of colour were cutting a giant swathe through the purplish-black mushrooming storm clouds—silver, livid green, molten gold and rose.

'Rambulara, the magic rainbow,' said Georgina.

They were still standing on the verandah when Quinn drove up. He gave Jill a friendly wave and called out to

Georgina, who had stayed at the house since her accident. 'Ready? No telling when this storm will hit.'

'Yes.' She ran back into the house to say goodbye to the children, kissed Jill on the cheek and climbed into the jeep. 'We've just seen your magic rainbow.'

'Rambulara?' He glanced at her briefly.

'It was beautiful.' There was an exquisite softness in her expression.

'Well, if you've seen it,' he said crisply, 'that means you can never leave me.'

But Georgina recoiled from his words and her face went a little white. Since the day of her accident new emotions had come into play between her and Quinn. So many things that they could never say to each other. Georgina yearned for things to be different, yet she felt curiously drained. Except for the odd moment, like now, Quinn too acted as though he no longer cared. Oh, not for her physical well-being—she could never accuse him of that. It was more as if both of them shared a sense of fatalism, the knowledge that they could never be together. Lucinda's destructive legacy.

Aunt Edwina's company was welcoming and peaceful, and Quinn excused himself straight after dinner to attend to some paper work.

'Remember it's your check-up tomorrow,' Aunt Edwina reminded Georgina before she retired. 'You and me.' She reached up and patted Georgina's face. You must be careful not to lose any more weight. You've lost quite enough already.'

When Georgina finally turned off her light lightning was forking across the sky, lighting it in jagged flashes but not one drop of rain had fallen. She opened out the french doors on to the verandah, thinking she could always close them when the rain came down. It was hard to shut out the streams of pungent air. She stood there for a moment clutching a vine-wreathed pillar, then she went back inside with the scent of king jasmine clinging to her robe and nightdress. As soon as Dr Moir gave her the all-clear she would have to return to her old life. It would be very, very difficult.

The storm hit an hour after midnight when most people on Rambulara station were deeply asleep. Dawn starts were the rule of the day so everyone was careful to get a good night's sleep. Georgina in her unhappiness and exhaustion was sleeping very deeply indeed.

The wind was driving from the north-east rattling all the shutters, and as it gathered in violence Georgina awoke with a gasp as the rain lashed in under the broad eaves and carried tingling spray right into the bedroom.

It seemed to take her ages to fight out of the mosquito netting, a huge lemon cloud that enfolded her, and now the wind was slashing at the long curtains lifting them and blowing them like shivery ghosts across the room.

'What the——' Quinn was striding swiftly around the verandah. Even from his own room he could hear the racket made by Georgina's open shutters. It was not possible that anyone could sleep so deeply. Or so he thought. One shutter had come away from its fastening and was flapping crazily. He caught it and pushed it in at the same time shooting the bolt.

'Oh, *Quinn!*' Georgina hurried out on to the verandah, sounding agonised and apologetic.

'Get inside,' he said shortly. 'You'll be soaked to the skin.'

'I don't care.' She was breathing in sharp little gasps. 'I should have closed these before I went to bed. *Oooh!*' The rain encompassed her, coiling around her warm body, a million tingles against her soft skin.

'I told you to stay inside.' Quinn slammed another pair of shutters closed.

'Damn it!' her eyes glittered. 'It's the rain. Don't you know what that means? It's rain. *Rain!*' Instead of seeking shelter she whirled out towards the lacy balustrade.

'Are you crazy?' Quinn looked after her.

'You tell me.' She lifted her arms to the storm-tossed sky. The rain was made of silver. It made her shiver.

'Come here,' he said harshly.

'I want to stand in the rain. Doesn't it smell exquisite?' She turned her slender body, her eyes huge and luminous in the dark.

'You're soaked, do you know that?' His voice sounded tight.

'I've got another nightgown.' She was shivery on the outside, yet her blood had turned to fire.

He pulled her to him and lifted her right off the polished floorboards, and it was then that she reached up blindly and pulled his head down to her. 'Kiss me.' Her voice sounded strange to her.

'Are you sure?'

She could feel the sharp reaction right through his body, the tremble in his strong arms.

'Make love to me in the rain,' she begged.

'And tomorrow?'

She shook her head, staring into his eyes. He was still wearing the clothes he had worn at dinner, which meant he hadn't even gone to bed, but her single garment was like oiled satin around her body. 'We might not have tomorrow,' she said chokingly.

'Little fool!' Quinn carried her inside the bedroom and held her, lowered to the floor, as he secured the remaining shutters.

Now the storm seemed far away and the room was very still and dark. Hunger presented itself, so deep and daring Georgina felt all her defences come tumbling down. She was aware of everything about him, his height and strength, his clean male scent, the warmth that was emanating from his body. She supposed she didn't just love him, she worshipped him. That seemed to be his gift.

'Damn it, where is it?' Quinn was muttering. He searched for and found the switch for the wall bracket.

'Did you *have* to do that?' she accused him fiercely. She turned her head away, but he still kept his arm around her locking her to his side.

'God, I could eat you,' he muttered. In one swift motion of surging blood he caught back her hair and gathered her into his arms, holding her so tightly there was nothing, absolutely nothing she could do. Desire was a tangible force and the light gleamed on her parted, waiting mouth.

Love me. *Love me*, she wanted to cry out flamboyantly, but he was reading every signal her yearning body was giving. He bowed his head and caught up her mouth; a kiss so demanding it was almost as if he was engaged in punishing her, and she, unaccountably, was submitting to this fierce onslaught.

Storm winds seemed to be blowing through her brain. She was totally receptive illuminated by emotions almost too strong for her fragile body. Quinn's hand was on her perfectly formed breast, at her narrow waist, slender hip, and she pressed her body against him, shuddering with this intimidating, intoxicating desire.

'You're burning, darling,' he whispered, his hand stroking her silky flesh, peeling a soft rouleau strap from her shoulder, cupping her naked breast, thumb and forefinger stimulating the rosy nipple to a superbly responsive peak. Georgina felt the convulsive repercussions right through her body and he drew back to look down on her, moisture sheening her porcelain skin, her long tawny hair darkened to wild honey.

His mind knew she could take a chill in her reduced, physical condition, but his body couldn't seem to accommodate anything else but his overriding desire to have her. He gathered her to him, breathing deeply, trying to control his spiralling senses. 'I should be drying you,' he murmured. 'I'm sure I should. Your hair is wet. So is your nightgown.'

'I don't care. Can't you see you've got me crazy? I *need* you so much!'

Obscurely that aroused a flicker of anger. 'What do you mean, need me? 'He bore her off towards the adjoining bathroom.

'Please,' she protested. 'I've needed you for a long time. Probably for ever.'

'That's why you've been such a cruel little bitch all this terrible week—cold, withdrawn, didn't want any part of me.' He grabbed two towels from a closet and draped them around her. 'Are you going to dry yourself, or am I?'

Her eyes flew to his, but he looked absolutely serious and resolute. 'Anyone would think I was going to catch pneumonia,' she said despairingly.

He merely shrugged moodily, watching the soft light reveal the frustration that was in her, the deep physical urgency. 'Be a good girl.'

'Oh, all right, then.' She padded into the bathroom and slammed the door. Her nightgown slid to the floor and she stood momentarily naked over the wet, crumpled satin. She felt like weeping at her appalling foolishness. What did she expect? That he would ravish her? No, he wouldn't, even when it suited her. She felt giddy with shame.

Abruptly she pulled one towel around her and rubbed her hair dry with the other. Or dry enough to satisfy him, she thought wildly. She would have to completely double think the whole damnable situation. She had thought him consumed with sensuality as she was, yet here he was acting the concerned adult to her breathless, abandoned adolescent. She wanted the most complete intimacy. He wanted her to avoid catching cold. It was the most dreadful, humiliating encounter that had ever taken place.

'Are you all right?' Quinn called sharply.

'Right as I'll ever be!' The towel around her was damp, so she reached for another from the closet. It was thick and fluffy and carried the lingering fragrance of boronia from one of the scented sachets. Her robe, as far as she could remember, was draped over the little powder-blue boudoir chair. Her hand on the crystal doorknob, she pulled the door open.

'So what next?' His beautiful mouth twisted at her

simmering expression, the wild heavy aureole of curls. She hadn't even bothered to draw a comb through them.

'Go away.' Her budding nipples were rubbing against the towel, the yearnings inside her so powerful she felt like clutching herself brokenly and moaning. 'Please, please, *please*!'

'What's so unbearable?' he demanded, giving her a very straight look. 'The thought of abandoning yourself to me, possible pregnancy, being misled, heartbreak, whatever? I hate to say this, Georgina, but you're a contrary little wretch.'

'Me? That's too much!' She made a movement to get past him and he shifted his tall, lean body out of the way. He looked completely self-possessed, whereas she looked and felt delirious. 'I think our little emergency might be over,' she said quickly, and picked up her robe.

'Let me help you.' Quick as a cat he was behind her. 'You look absolutely stunning in peach satin.' He gripped her shoulders, his fingers exploring the delicate bones and hollows, sensations going all the way to her toes.

Georgina jerked away and as she did so, stumbled over the Persian rug. 'You brute!' she muttered.

'That's good.' He didn't even have to work hard to scoop her up. She might have been Melissa's age. 'I'll go,' he said, 'but not before you tell me you love me.'

'What, again?

'What do you mean, *again*? I've never heard it once.' He almost threw her on to the bed where she lay panting while he leaned over her.

'I'm terrified of you, do you know that?' Georgina put her hands to her temples, then flipped over on her side. 'I've never felt like this in my entire life.'

'Surprise, surprise, I haven't either.' He sat down near her curling toes and when she didn't move he leaned over and finally slid down alongside her. 'Come on, little one, stop shaking.' He pulled her, still trembling, into his arms.

It occurred to her for the first time that it wasn't only passion he felt for her. It was real love. She could feel the protection in his strong arms, the total commitment. He's really incapable of hurting me, Georgina thought.

He was kissing her eyelids, her temples, beneath her ears and her chin, her quivering mouth. 'Do you want this to go any further?' he murmured. 'Georgina, look at me.'

'I think so. Perhaps for a little while.' Tentatively she began to kiss him back—a delirious pleasure. 'You make me feel so much. It's almost scary, like a ritual. Yet we're only kissing.'

'Yes, we're only kissing,' Quinn moved his mouth up and over hers.

'You really love me, don't you?' A tear slid out of her eye.

'I love you so much I'm even prepared to get up.'

'I suppose we should,' she sighed deeply, lacking the ability to do anything about it.

'If that towel comes down any further all my good intentions will go for nothing,' he told her.

'Will they?'

'Yes. Absolutely.'

Georgina drew herself up on her elbows. 'Will Lucinda ever come back?' she asked poignantly.

'My God!' Quinn rolled back and shut his eyes. 'Do we really have to speak about that dreadful woman? If my suspicions are correct, she's going to end up in an asylum.'

'You were very good to her,' she admitted.

'Oh, shut up,' he groaned. 'Good to her! She sure showed her gratitude.'

'And I'm no substitute?'

'Oh, you lunatic!' His chest heaved and he pulled her down to him. 'You're everything I ever dreamed about. You're exquisite. Had I made you myself I couldn't love you more. Now will you *please shut up*!'

More lover-like words couldn't have gladdened her heart more, 'I love you, Quinn,' she said fervently. 'I've loved you right from that very first day. What do they say? A bolt from the blue!'

He smiled and his eyes were as brilliant as sapphires. 'I understand. I'm going to kiss you one more time, just for an instant, then I'm going to get up.'

'You mean you think we should be churched first?'

'Urgently. I don't want to do a thing wrong. Nothing. Not the slightest thing to hurt you. You're mine now and I'm going to look after you for ever.'

'How did you get in here anyway!' Georgina smiled. 'I can't remember.'

He pulled her towards him, fitting her close to his body. 'Oh, you remember all right. I'm the honourable one around here.'

'Thank God!' she sighed.

'I won't keep you long.' He brushed his lips against her, then kissed her urgently, not using his hands at all. 'All right, that's it!' he said thickly, and heaved himself off the bed. 'In three weeks, four, you'll be happily married, Miss Hamilton. I'll get on to Judge Coleman first thing in the morning. Agreed?'

'Agreed.' Her face was illuminated with the force of her love.

Quinn half turned and looked at her, 'My God, but you'll make a beautiful bride!'

His arm came up determinedly to open the french doors. Outside the reign of the storm was over, but the rain was still falling in straight, drumming splendour.

Georgina was still sitting perfectly still on the bed, her face meltingly soft and radiant within the luxuriant, tousled frame of her hair.

'You can see what it's going to be like, can't you?'

'Precisely why I'm ringing the judge in the morning. If we give it a month that will allow all the family time to arrive.'

'A month, then,' she whispered. 'And no more.'

'A small price to pay, with a whole lifetime to share.'

Take these 4 best-selling novels FREE

Yes! Four sophisticated, contemporary love stories by four world-famous authors of romance FREE, as your introduction to the Harlequin Presents subscription plan. Thrill to **Anne Mather**'s passionate story BORN OUT OF LOVE, set in the Caribbean.... Travel to darkest Africa in **Violet Winspear**'s TIME OF THE TEMPTRESS....Let **Charlotte Lamb** take you to the fascinating world of London's Fleet Street in MAN'S WORLD.... Discover beautiful Greece in **Sally Wentworth**'s moving romance SAY HELLO TO YESTERDAY.

Harlequin Presents...

The very finest in romance fiction

Join the millions of avid Harlequin readers all over the world who delight in the magic of a really exciting novel. EIGHT great NEW titles published EACH MONTH! Each month you will get to know exciting, interesting, true-to-life people .... You'll be swept to distant lands you've dreamed of visiting .... Intrigue, adventure, romance, and the destiny of many lives will thrill you through each Harlequin Presents novel.

Get all the latest books before they're sold out!
As a Harlequin subscriber you actually receive your personal copies of the latest Presents novels immediately after they come off the press, so you're sure of getting all 8 each month.

Cancel your subscription whenever you wish!
You don't have to buy any minimum number of books. Whenever you decide to stop your subscription just let us know and we'll cancel all further shipments.